ArtScroll Youth Series

Rabbi Nosson Scherman / Rabbi Meir Zlotowitz

General Editors

THE PERITZ EDITION

הדרך השלישי

Published by

Mesorah Publications, ltd

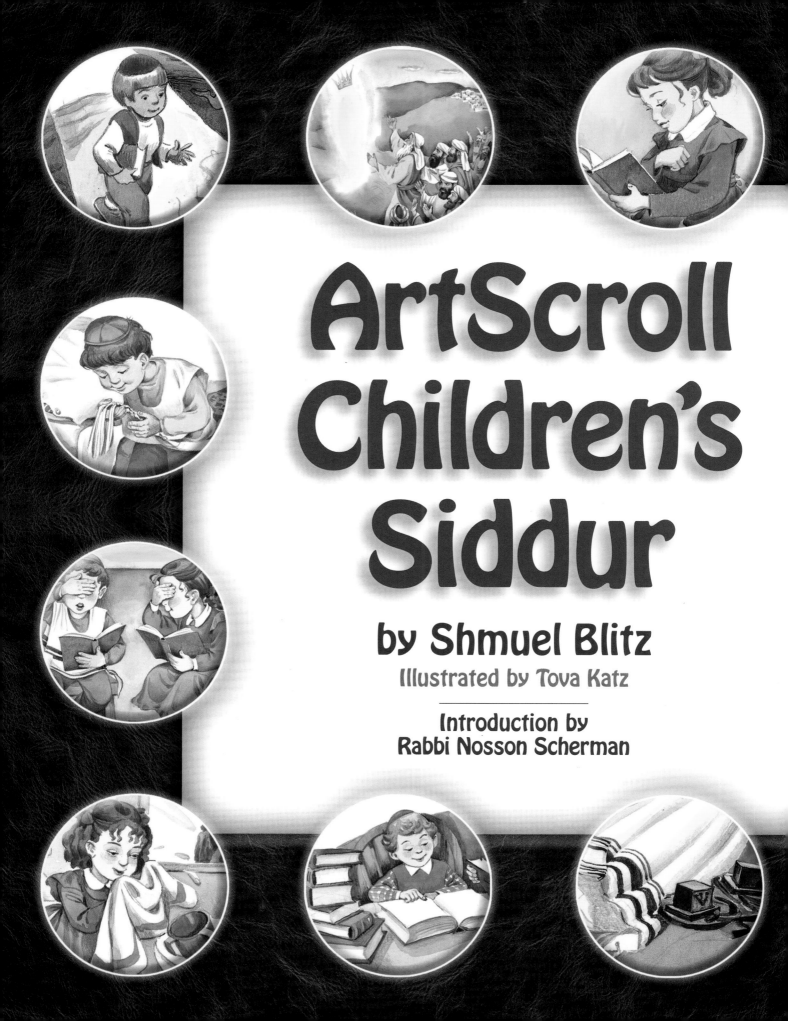

ArtScroll Children's Siddur

by Shmuel Blitz

Illustrated by Tova Katz

Introduction by
Rabbi Nosson Scherman

This Siddur is dedicated in memory of

Rabbi Yisroel Yehudah Peritz זצ״ל

הרב הגאון רבי ישראל יהודה ב״ר יוסף זצ״ל

נפטר י״ד אייר פסח שני תשל״ה

Rebbetzin Martha Peritz ע״ה

הרבנית מרת מינדל בת הר״ר יהודה דוד גולדשמידט ע״ה

נפטרה י״ח תשרי ב׳ דחוה״מ סוכות תש״ס

Their parents were proud and inspiring examples of the *Torah im Derech Eretz* of Rabbiner Hirsch, and they inherited that *mesiras nefesh* for Torah and truth.

Born in Breslau, RABBI PERITZ became not only a talmid muvhak of Rabbi Akiva Schreiber in Pressburg, but they maintained a lifelong close relationship. Later, as the Rav of Marburg, Germany, he was the spiritual leader of forty congregations, which he served with loyalty and distinction.

When he had the chance to leave Nazi Germany, he refused, saying, "How can I go when my people need me most?" A survivor of Buchenwald, he came to England and then America. In Chicago, he founded a kehillah and had a profound effect on people of many ages and backgrounds, as a teacher and role model.

After a short stay in Israel, he retired to Manchester, where he taught and studied Torah to the end of his enormously productive life.

REBBETZIN PERITZ was born in Schluchtern near Frankfurt, where her father was the *parnes*. The kindness, charity, modesty, and sense of communal responsibility of her family remained with her always.

Anyone who saw her *daven* could not fail to be moved. Her regal spirit triumphed over hardship and ill health, as she supported her husband's work and made her teaching and nurturing of Jewish children the focus of her public life.

To Rabbi and Rebbetzin Peritz nothing was more important than bringing the joy of Judaism to Jews — especially the young. How appropriate, therefore, that this Siddur, which will do what they did, should be dedicated to their memory.

ת נ צ ב ה

FIRST EDITION *Nine Impressions … June 2001 — September 2014*
ARTSCROLL® SERIES / ARTSCROLL CHILDREN'S SIDDUR — THE PERITZ EDITION
© Copyright 2001, by MESORAH PUBLICATIONS, Ltd., 4401 Second Avenue / Brooklyn, NY 11232 / (718) 921-9000 / www.artscroll.com

ISBN 10: 1-57819-564-0 / ISBN 13: 978-1-57819-564-0
Typography by CompuScribe at ArtScroll Studios, Ltd.
Printed in the USA by Noble Book Press.

Table of Contents

Introduction

Prayer — Our Connection to Hashem

There are three partners in every child: the father, the mother, and Hashem. We see our parents all the time, but what about Hashem? We don't see Him, even though we know that He is the One Who gave us our *neshamah* and keeps us alive.

Just as we try to be close to our parents, we should try to be close to Hashem and do what He wants us to. We know that Hashem wants us to be good and to make ourselves better all the time. How can we do that?

One way is to thank Him for all the good things He gives us. When we pray to Hashem and really think about the prayers, we do that. If we understand what we are saying, the Siddur brings us closer to Him.

That is what we hope this Siddur will do. We want you to use it and enjoy it. Most of all, we hope that it will help you learn how good it is to pray to Hashem and become better Jews.

Asking Hashem

WHEN WE NEED SOMETHING FROM OUR PARENTS, we can ask them for it. There are also lots of things we need from Hashem. We want good health for ourselves and our families, we want to learn well, we want everyone to like us, we want Mashiach to come — we want all kinds of good things. How do we ask Hashem for something? The answer is simple. We open our Siddur and speak to Him.

Our Telephone to Hashem

THE TORAH TELLS US THAT WHEN WE *DAVEN* (PRAY), we are serving Hashem with our hearts. That means that we think about Him and feel in our hearts how much we should thank Him for all the good things He gives us. We know that only He can give us all the things we want, and really need. When we pray, we are speaking to Hashem, and we are reminding ourselves that Hashem loves us and wants to help us be good. You can even say that our Siddur is like a telephone to Hashem. We can talk directly to Him. *We* can't hear *Him*, but *He* hears every word we say.

When and Where

WE CAN ALWAYS PRAY TO HASHEM — AND WE *SHOULD!* If someone is sick or if we are in trouble, we should ask Hashem for help. If something good happens, we should thank Hashem. Really, we should *always* thank Him for things like a good family, good health, or good friends.

Besides this, our rabbis set special times to pray every day. Even when we are very young, we *daven Shacharis* every morning. As we get older, we *daven Minchah* in the afternoon, and *Maariv* at night. We say *Shema* before we go to sleep. Before we eat we say a *berachah*, thanking Hashem for the food. When we finish eating, we thank Him again.

The best place for the regular prayers is in shul, with a *minyan*. If we can't go to shul, we should pray at home, or wherever we are.

Does Hashem Answer Our Prayers?

YES. ALWAYS. BUT SOMETIMES HIS ANSWER IS NO. Why doesn't He always want us to have the things we want very much? Let's imagine that someone prays to eat ice cream and candy all day long. Or that someone prays that he or she should be able to run away from home and join the circus. Should Hashem say yes to such prayers? Of course not, because such things are bad for us. Hashem loves us very much, and does not want us to have things that are not good for us.

Hashem is the only one who knows what is best for us. If we ask for the wrong thing, He will change it to something good. Sometimes, we don't understand what is good for us and what is bad — but Hashem knows.

A very sad woman once came to a rabbi. She asked him why Hashem let her husband die. She had *davened* so much and cried so much for him to get better. Why were her prayers wasted? The rabbi answered, "Hashem *did* hear your prayers. Your prayers were *not* wasted. Maybe because of your prayers, someone else's little girl got well, or someone else's husband was able to get a good job. No prayer is ever wasted."

Then the woman understood how important her prayers are. She smiled for the first time since her husband got sick.

We hope this Siddur will help you *daven* to Hashem. He loves you and He loves your prayers. He wants you to love saying them as much as He loves hearing them. This Siddur will be your best friend. May it help you on the road to becoming a wonderful servant of Hashem.

Tammuz 5761/June 2001   **Rabbi Nosson Scherman**

The author dedicates his work to the memory of his father-in-law,

Mr. Harold Hoenig ❖ צבי אריה בן משה הכהן ז״ל

מוֹדֶה אֲנִי / Modeh Ani

When we wake up in the morning, the first thing we do is thank Hashem for giving us one more day of life.

מוֹדֶה אֲנִי לְפָנֶיךָ, מֶלֶךְ חַי וְקַיָּם
שֶׁהֶחֱזַרְתָּ בִּי נִשְׁמָתִי בְּחֶמְלָה – רַבָּה אֱמוּנָתֶךָ.

I thank You, Hashem, because You have kindly given me back my soul.

We then wash our hands as follows: First, hold a cup with the right hand and fill it with water. Then, pass the cup to the left hand. Pour water over the right hand. Then, take the cup in the right hand, and pour water over the left hand. Keep doing this until the water has been poured over each hand three times. We then say:

רֵאשִׁית חָכְמָה יִרְאַת יהוה, שֵׂכֶל טוֹב לְכָל עֹשֵׂיהֶם, תְּהִלָּתוֹ עֹמֶדֶת לָעַד.
בָּרוּךְ שֵׁם כְּבוֹד מַלְכוּתוֹ לְעוֹלָם וָעֶד.

In order for someone to be a wise person, first he must fear Hashem,
Whose praise lasts forever.
Blessed is the Name of His wonderful Kingdom forever and ever.

Did You Know??
We can say *Modeh Ani* as soon as we wake up, even before we wash our hands, because the Name of Hashem is not mentioned.

A Closer Look
It is only because of Hashem's kindness and goodness that we wake up each morning. We wake up every day ready to serve Hashem and do His mitzvos.

לְבִישַׁת צִיצָת / **Putting on Tzitzis**

(This mitzvah is for boys.)

We take the *tallis katan* and check to make sure the *tzitzis* are not torn. Then we say:

Blessed are You, Hashem, our God, King of the universe, Who has made us holy with His mitzvos, and commanded us about the mitzvah of *tzitzis*.

בָּרוּךְ אַתָּה יהוה אֱלֹהֵינוּ מֶלֶךְ הָעוֹלָם, אֲשֶׁר קִדְּשָׁנוּ בְּמִצְוֹתָיו, וְצִוָּנוּ עַל מִצְוַת צִיצָת.

Now put on the *tallis katan*. If someone wears a *tallis* during *Shacharis*, he does not say this *berachah* now, but says a *berachah* when he puts on his *tallis*.

מַה טֹבוּ / *Mah Tovu*

מַה טֹבוּ אֹהָלֶיךָ יַעֲקֹב, מִשְׁכְּנֹתֶיךָ יִשְׂרָאֵל. וַאֲנִי בְּרֹב חַסְדְּךָ אָבוֹא בֵיתֶךָ, אֶשְׁתַּחֲוֶה אֶל הֵיכַל קָדְשְׁךָ בְּיִרְאָתֶךָ. יהוה, אָהַבְתִּי מְעוֹן בֵּיתֶךָ, וּמְקוֹם מִשְׁכַּן כְּבוֹדֶךָ. וַאֲנִי אֶשְׁתַּחֲוֶה וְאֶכְרָעָה, אֶבְרְכָה לִפְנֵי יהוה עֹשִׂי. וַאֲנִי, תְפִלָּתִי לְךָ יהוה, עֵת רָצוֹן; אֱלֹהִים, בְּרָב חַסְדֶּךָ, עֲנֵנִי בֶּאֱמֶת יִשְׁעֶךָ.

The tents of the Jewish people are so good! (Our "tents" are the shuls where we learn and pray.) You are so kind for allowing me to come to shul and pray. I will bow down in front of You because I fear You. I love Your House of Prayer, where You are. Please accept my prayer, Hashem. And please answer me and help me.

Did You Know??

King Balak hired Bil'am to curse the Jewish people. Bil'am was a very bad person. He kept trying to curse the Jews, but Hashem would not let him. When Bil'am tried to curse them, he saw how holy the Jewish people were. Even their tent openings did not face each other, allowing for more modesty between the people. All Bil'am could say was *Mah Tovu*, how good they are.

A Closer Look

Hashem loves us and wants to hear our prayers every day. He wants us to speak to Him and be close to Him.

Adon Olam / אֲדוֹן עוֹלָם

In *Adon Olam* we say that Hashem always was, always is, and always will be.
He is all-powerful and can do anything and everything. And He is always very close to us.

Master of the universe,
    Who was always King,
      even before anything was created.

When nothing will exist anymore,
    only He will rule.

Hashem always was here,
    Hashem always is here,
    and Hashem will always
      be here.

Hashem is the only One,
    there is no other god.

Hashem has no beginning
    and no end,
      Hashem is amazingly strong.

Hashem is my God, and my Redeemer,
    He helps me in my times of trouble.

I am safe with Him,
    He is there when I call to Him.

He watches over my soul
    when I go to sleep,
      and when I wake up in the morning.

Hashem is always with me,
    and I shall not be afraid.

אֲדוֹן עוֹלָם אֲשֶׁר מָלַךְ,
בְּטֶרֶם כָּל־יְצִיר נִבְרָא.
לְעֵת נַעֲשָׂה בְחֶפְצוֹ כֹּל,
אֲזַי מֶלֶךְ שְׁמוֹ נִקְרָא.
וְאַחֲרֵי כִּכְלוֹת הַכֹּל,
לְבַדּוֹ יִמְלוֹךְ נוֹרָא.
וְהוּא הָיָה וְהוּא הֹוֶה,
וְהוּא יִהְיֶה בְּתִפְאָרָה.
וְהוּא אֶחָד וְאֵין שֵׁנִי,
לְהַמְשִׁיל לוֹ לְהַחְבִּירָה.
בְּלִי רֵאשִׁית בְּלִי תַכְלִית,
וְלוֹ הָעֹז וְהַמִּשְׂרָה.
וְהוּא אֵלִי וְחַי גֹּאֲלִי,
וְצוּר חֶבְלִי בְּעֵת צָרָה.
וְהוּא נִסִּי וּמָנוֹס לִי,
מְנָת כּוֹסִי בְּיוֹם אֶקְרָא.
בְּיָדוֹ אַפְקִיד רוּחִי,
בְּעֵת אִישַׁן וְאָעִירָה.
וְעִם רוּחִי גְּוִיָּתִי,
יהוה לִי וְלֹא אִירָא.

Did You Know??
When we pray, we are speaking directly with Hashem.
The highest level of prayer a person can reach is to pray like a young child.

A Closer Look
We are never really alone. Hashem is always with us. We can always talk directly to Him by praying.

יִגְדַּל / Yigdal

Yigdal describes the *Rambam*'s Thirteen Basic Ideas of Faith.
These are the 13 principles that we are all required to believe.

1. Hashem is great, He is to be praised,
   He is always there.
2. He is the only One —
   there is no other god,
   He is forever.

יִגְדַּל אֱלֹהִים חַי וְיִשְׁתַּבַּח,
נִמְצָא וְאֵין עֵת אֶל מְצִיאוּתוֹ.
אֶחָד וְאֵין יָחִיד כְּיִחוּדוֹ,
נֶעְלָם וְגַם אֵין סוֹף לְאַחְדּוּתוֹ.

3. He has no body and He has no shape.
   Nothing can be compared to Him.
4. He was there
   before anything was created;
   He was first,
   there was nothing before Him.
5. He is Ruler over everything,
   and He shows His greatness
   and Kingship.
6. He has given prophecy to the Jews,
   His chosen people.
7. There was never another prophet
   like Moshe,
   a prophet who saw everything
   so clearly.
8. Hashem has given His Torah
   to the Jewish people
   through His prophet, Moshe.
9. Hashem will never change His laws.
10. He always knows
    what we are thinking;
    He knows everything
    that will happen.
11. He gives people reward
    for what they do,
    but a wicked person is punished
    for the evil he has done.
12. In the future,
    He will send the Mashiach
    to redeem everyone
    who waited for him.
13. Hashem will bring the dead
    back to life.
    Blessed is His Name forever.

אֵין לוֹ דְמוּת הַגּוּף וְאֵינוֹ גוּף,

לֹא נַעֲרוֹךְ אֵלָיו קְדֻשָּׁתוֹ.

קַדְמוֹן לְכָל דָּבָר אֲשֶׁר נִבְרָא,

רִאשׁוֹן וְאֵין רֵאשִׁית לְרֵאשִׁיתוֹ.

הִנּוֹ אֲדוֹן עוֹלָם לְכָל נוֹצָר,

יוֹרֶה גְדֻלָּתוֹ וּמַלְכוּתוֹ.

שֶׁפַע נְבוּאָתוֹ נְתָנוֹ,

אֶל אַנְשֵׁי סְגֻלָּתוֹ וְתִפְאַרְתּוֹ.

לֹא קָם בְּיִשְׂרָאֵל כְּמֹשֶׁה עוֹד,

נָבִיא וּמַבִּיט אֶת תְּמוּנָתוֹ.

תּוֹרַת אֱמֶת נָתַן לְעַמּוֹ אֵל,

עַל יַד נְבִיאוֹ נֶאֱמַן בֵּיתוֹ.

לֹא יַחֲלִיף הָאֵל וְלֹא יָמִיר דָּתוֹ,

לְעוֹלָמִים לְזוּלָתוֹ.

צוֹפֶה וְיוֹדֵעַ סְתָרֵינוּ,

מַבִּיט לְסוֹף דָּבָר בְּקַדְמָתוֹ.

גּוֹמֵל לְאִישׁ חֶסֶד כְּמִפְעָלוֹ,

נוֹתֵן לְרָשָׁע רָע כְּרִשְׁעָתוֹ.

יִשְׁלַח לְקֵץ הַיָּמִין מְשִׁיחֵנוּ,

לִפְדּוֹת מְחַכֵּי קֵץ יְשׁוּעָתוֹ.

מֵתִים יְחַיֶּה אֵל בְּרֹב חַסְדּוֹ,

בָּרוּךְ עֲדֵי עַד שֵׁם תְּהִלָּתוֹ.

Did You Know??
Hashem does not need our prayers, but we need to pray to Him. We need to be closer to Hashem. That is what our soul desires.

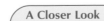

A Closer Look
Hashem always answers our prayers. But sometimes His answer is "no." Only Hashem knows what is best for us. He knows that sometimes it is better for us not to get something that we ask for.

נְטִילַת יָדַיִם / Netilas Yadayim

Even though we washed our hands and went to the bathroom when we woke up,
many people say the *berachos* now so that these *berachos* will be said at *Shacharis*.

Blessed are You, Hashem, our God, King of the universe, Who has made us holy with His mitzvos, and commanded us about washing our hands.

בָּרוּךְ אַתָּה יהוה אֱלֹהֵינוּ מֶלֶךְ הָעוֹלָם, אֲשֶׁר קִדְּשָׁנוּ בְּמִצְוֹתָיו, וְצִוָּנוּ עַל נְטִילַת יָדָיִם.

אֲשֶׁר יָצַר / Asher Yatzar

Blessed are You, Hashem, our God, King of the universe, Who has made man with wisdom. You created man with a body that works so well. You know that if even one part of our body is blocked and does not work properly, it would be impossible for us to live. Blessed are You, Hashem, Who heals people and does wondrous things.

בָּרוּךְ אַתָּה יהוה אֱלֹהֵינוּ מֶלֶךְ הָעוֹלָם, אֲשֶׁר יָצַר אֶת הָאָדָם בְּחָכְמָה, וּבָרָא בוֹ נְקָבִים נְקָבִים, חֲלוּלִים חֲלוּלִים. גָּלוּי וְיָדוּעַ לִפְנֵי כִסֵּא כְבוֹדֶךָ, שֶׁאִם יִפָּתֵחַ אֶחָד מֵהֶם, אוֹ יִסָּתֵם אֶחָד מֵהֶם, אִי אֶפְשָׁר לְהִתְקַיֵּם וְלַעֲמוֹד לְפָנֶיךָ. בָּרוּךְ אַתָּה יהוה, רוֹפֵא כָל בָּשָׂר וּמַפְלִיא לַעֲשׂוֹת.

A Closer Look
Our bodies are so complicated. If even one part of our bodies did not work the right way, we could become very sick. In the blessing *Asher Yatzar*, we thank Hashem for making our bodies work.

Did You Know??
Every day we should recite at least 100 blessings. The first of these blessings is *Al Netilas Yadayim*.

Some say אֱלֹהַי נְשָׁמָה (on page 15) now.

בִּרְכוֹת הַתּוֹרָה / Blessings on the Torah

One of the first things we do every morning is thank Hashem for giving us His Torah and letting us learn it.

Blessed are You, Hashem, our God, King of the universe, Who has made us holy with His mitzvos, and has commanded us to learn Torah. And please, Hashem, make the Torah pleasant to us, and to all of Your people. May we and our children understand You and study Your Torah simply because You told us to study it. Blessed are You, Hashem, Who teaches Torah to His nation, Israel.

בָּרוּךְ אַתָּה יהוה אֱלֹהֵינוּ מֶלֶךְ הָעוֹלָם, אֲשֶׁר קִדְּשָׁנוּ בְּמִצְוֹתָיו, וְצִוָּנוּ לַעֲסוֹק בְּדִבְרֵי תוֹרָה. וְהַעֲרֶב נָא יהוה אֱלֹהֵינוּ אֶת דִּבְרֵי תוֹרָתְךָ בְּפִינוּ וּבְפִי עַמְּךָ בֵּית יִשְׂרָאֵל. וְנִהְיֶה אֲנַחְנוּ וְצֶאֱצָאֵינוּ וְצֶאֱצָאֵי עַמְּךָ בֵּית יִשְׂרָאֵל, כֻּלָּנוּ יוֹדְעֵי שְׁמֶךָ וְלוֹמְדֵי תוֹרָתֶךָ לִשְׁמָהּ. בָּרוּךְ אַתָּה יהוה, הַמְלַמֵּד תּוֹרָה לְעַמּוֹ יִשְׂרָאֵל.

Blessed are You, Hashem, our God, King of the universe, Who chose us from all the other nations, and gave us His Torah. Blessed are You, Hashem, Who gives the Torah.

בָּרוּךְ אַתָּה יהוה אֱלֹהֵינוּ מֶלֶךְ הָעוֹלָם, אֲשֶׁר בָּחַר בָּנוּ מִכָּל הָעַמִּים וְנָתַן לָנוּ אֶת תּוֹרָתוֹ. בָּרוּךְ אַתָּה יהוה, נוֹתֵן הַתּוֹרָה.

After making this *berachah,* we say these verses from the Torah.

May Hashem bless you, and watch over you. May the Light of Hashem shine upon you. May Hashem look favorably on you, and bring you peace.

יְבָרֶכְךָ יהוה וְיִשְׁמְרֶךָ. יָאֵר יהוה פָּנָיו אֵלֶיךָ וִיחֻנֶּךָּ. יִשָּׂא יהוה פָּנָיו אֵלֶיךָ, וְיָשֵׂם לְךָ שָׁלוֹם.

A Closer Look

Learning Torah is the most important commandment Hashem has given us. Our Sages teach us that without Torah we are like fish without water; the Jewish people would not be able to survive. When we say that we study Torah "simply because You told us to study it," we mean that we study Torah not for honor, profit, or because our parents and teachers tell us to. We do it to please Hashem and in order to know His Torah. This is called learning Torah "lishmah."

אֱלֹהַי נְשָׁמָה / Elohai Neshamah

My God, the soul that you put inside me is pure. You made it, You breathed it into me. You take care of it while it is in me. Some day You will take it back from me, and will give it back to me again in the future. As long as my soul is within me, I thank You, Hashem, My God, the God of my fathers, Ruler of everything, Lord of all souls. Blessed are You, Hashem, who returns people's souls to their bodies.

אֱלֹהַי, נְשָׁמָה שֶׁנָּתַתָּ בִּי טְהוֹרָה הִיא. אַתָּה בְרָאתָהּ אַתָּה יְצַרְתָּהּ, אַתָּה נְפַחְתָּהּ בִּי, וְאַתָּה מְשַׁמְּרָהּ בְּקִרְבִּי, וְאַתָּה עָתִיד לִטְּלָהּ מִמֶּנִּי, וּלְהַחֲזִירָהּ בִּי לֶעָתִיד לָבֹא. כָּל זְמַן שֶׁהַנְּשָׁמָה בְקִרְבִּי, מוֹדֶה אֲנִי לְפָנֶיךָ, יהוה אֱלֹהַי וֵאלֹהֵי אֲבוֹתַי, רִבּוֹן כָּל הַמַּעֲשִׂים, אֲדוֹן כָּל הַנְּשָׁמוֹת. בָּרוּךְ אַתָּה יהוה, הַמַּחֲזִיר נְשָׁמוֹת לִפְגָרִים מֵתִים.

A Closer Look

This prayer shows how close we feel to Hashem. We thank Him for letting us wake up every morning. Just as Hashem is always pure, our soul, which is a gift from Him, always remains pure.

בִּרְכוֹת הַשַּׁחַר / *Morning Blessings*

In the following blessings we thank Hashem for the pleasures
He allows us to enjoy each and every day.

בָּרוּךְ אַתָּה יהוה אֱלֹהֵינוּ מֶלֶךְ הָעוֹלָם,
אֲשֶׁר נָתַן לַשֶּׂכְוִי בִינָה לְהַבְחִין
בֵּין יוֹם וּבֵין לָיְלָה.

Blessed are You, Hashem, our God, King of the
universe, Who lets us understand the difference
between day and night.

בָּרוּךְ אַתָּה יהוה אֱלֹהֵינוּ מֶלֶךְ הָעוֹלָם,
שֶׁלֹּא עָשַׂנִי גּוֹי.

Blessed are You, Hashem, our God, King of the
universe, for not making me a non-Jew.

בָּרוּךְ אַתָּה יהוה אֱלֹהֵינוּ מֶלֶךְ הָעוֹלָם,
שֶׁלֹּא עָשַׂנִי עָבֶד.

Blessed are You, Hashem, our God, King of the
universe, for not making me a slave.

BOYS SAY:

בָּרוּךְ אַתָּה יהוה אֱלֹהֵינוּ מֶלֶךְ הָעוֹלָם,
שֶׁלֹּא עָשַׂנִי אִשָּׁה.

Blessed are You, Hashem, our God, King of the
universe, for not making me a woman.

GIRLS SAY:

בָּרוּךְ אַתָּה יהוה אֱלֹהֵינוּ מֶלֶךְ הָעוֹלָם,
שֶׁעָשַׂנִי כִּרְצוֹנוֹ.

Blessed are You, Hashem, our God, King of the
universe, for making me the way You wanted.

16

בָּרוּךְ אַתָּה יהוה אֱלֹהֵינוּ מֶלֶךְ הָעוֹלָם,
פּוֹקֵחַ עִוְרִים.

Blessed are You, Hashem, our God, King of the universe, Who makes the blind able to see.

בָּרוּךְ אַתָּה יהוה אֱלֹהֵינוּ מֶלֶךְ הָעוֹלָם,
מַלְבִּישׁ עֲרֻמִּים.

Blessed are You, Hashem, our God, King of the universe, Who gives us clothing.

בָּרוּךְ אַתָּה יהוה אֱלֹהֵינוּ מֶלֶךְ הָעוֹלָם,
מַתִּיר אֲסוּרִים.

Blessed are You, Hashem, our God, King of the universe, Who frees people who are tied up.

בָּרוּךְ אַתָּה יהוה אֱלֹהֵינוּ מֶלֶךְ הָעוֹלָם,
זוֹקֵף כְּפוּפִים.

Blessed are You, Hashem, our God, King of the universe, Who straightens out people who are bent.

בָּרוּךְ אַתָּה יהוה אֱלֹהֵינוּ מֶלֶךְ הָעוֹלָם,
רוֹקַע הָאָרֶץ עַל הַמָּיִם.

Blessed are You, Hashem, our God, King of the universe, Who spreads the earth over the waters.

A Closer Look

Men are responsible to do more mitzvos than women, while women are the foundation and support of the Jewish home.

בָּרוּךְ אַתָּה יהוה אֱלֹהֵינוּ מֶלֶךְ הָעוֹלָם,
שֶׁעָשָׂה לִי כָּל צָרְכִּי.

Blessed are You, Hashem, our God, King of the universe, Who takes care of all my needs.

בָּרוּךְ אַתָּה יהוה אֱלֹהֵינוּ מֶלֶךְ הָעוֹלָם,
הַמֵּכִין מִצְעֲדֵי גָבֶר.

Blessed are You, Hashem, our God, King of the universe, Who takes care of every step I take.

בָּרוּךְ אַתָּה יהוה אֱלֹהֵינוּ מֶלֶךְ הָעוֹלָם,
אוֹזֵר יִשְׂרָאֵל בִּגְבוּרָה.

Blessed are You, Hashem, our God, King of the universe, Who gives the nation of Israel the strength it needs.

בָּרוּךְ אַתָּה יהוה אֱלֹהֵינוּ מֶלֶךְ הָעוֹלָם,
עוֹטֵר יִשְׂרָאֵל בְּתִפְאָרָה.

Blessed are You, Hashem, our God, King of the universe, Who crowns the nation of Israel with splendor.

בָּרוּךְ אַתָּה יהוה אֱלֹהֵינוּ מֶלֶךְ הָעוֹלָם,
הַנּוֹתֵן לַיָּעֵף כֹּחַ.

Blessed are You, Hashem, our God, King of the universe, Who gives strength to the tired.

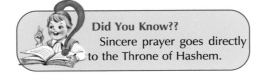

Did You Know??
Sincere prayer goes directly to the Throne of Hashem.

Blessed are You, Hashem, our God, King of the universe, Who removes the sleep from my eyes. And please help us learn Your Torah and do Your mitzvos. Do not let us commit sins, and do not give us choices that are too difficult. Do not let us be embarrassed. Do not let the *yetzer hara* be too strong for us, and keep us away from bad people and bad friends. Let the *yetzer hatov* influence us to do good deeds. Every day show us Your kindness and mercy. Blessed are You, Hashem, Who does good things for His people, Israel.

בָּרוּךְ אַתָּה יהוה אֱלֹהֵינוּ מֶלֶךְ הָעוֹלָם, הַמַּעֲבִיר שֵׁנָה מֵעֵינָי וּתְנוּמָה מֵעַפְעַפָּי. וִיהִי רָצוֹן מִלְּפָנֶיךָ, יהוה אֱלֹהֵינוּ וֵאלֹהֵי אֲבוֹתֵינוּ, שֶׁתַּרְגִּילֵנוּ בְּתוֹרָתֶךָ וְדַבְּקֵנוּ בְּמִצְוֹתֶיךָ, וְאַל תְּבִיאֵנוּ לֹא לִידֵי חֵטְא, וְלֹא לִידֵי עֲבֵרָה וְעָוֹן, וְלֹא לִידֵי נִסָּיוֹן, וְלֹא לִידֵי בִזָּיוֹן, וְאַל תַּשְׁלֶט בָּנוּ יֵצֶר הָרָע. וְהַרְחִיקֵנוּ מֵאָדָם רָע וּמֵחָבֵר רָע. וְדַבְּקֵנוּ בְּיֵצֶר הַטּוֹב וּבְמַעֲשִׂים טוֹבִים, וְכוֹף אֶת יִצְרֵנוּ לְהִשְׁתַּעְבֶּד לָךְ. וּתְנֵנוּ הַיּוֹם וּבְכָל יוֹם לְחֵן וּלְחֶסֶד וּלְרַחֲמִים בְּעֵינֶיךָ, וּבְעֵינֵי כָל רוֹאֵינוּ, וְתִגְמְלֵנוּ חֲסָדִים טוֹבִים. בָּרוּךְ אַתָּה יהוה, גוֹמֵל חֲסָדִים טוֹבִים לְעַמּוֹ יִשְׂרָאֵל.

A Closer Look

Even if a person does not understand the exact meaning of each word of the prayers, sincere prayers still reach the Gates of Heaven.

We thank Hashem for letting us serve Him and do His mitzvos.

May it be Your desire, Hashem, my God, and the God of my fathers, that You save me each day from disrespectful people and from being disrespectful; from bad people and bad friends and bad neighbors; from bad things happening to me; from the evil inclination and from strict judgment. Also, save me from having to deal with any difficult people.

יְהִי רָצוֹן מִלְּפָנֶיךָ, יהוה אֱלֹהַי וֵאלֹהֵי אֲבוֹתַי, שֶׁתַּצִּילֵנִי הַיּוֹם וּבְכָל יוֹם מֵעַזֵּי פָנִים וּמֵעַזּוּת פָּנִים, מֵאָדָם רָע, וּמֵחָבֵר רָע, וּמִשָּׁכֵן רָע, וּמִפֶּגַע רָע, וּמִשָּׂטָן הַמַּשְׁחִית, מִדִּין קָשֶׁה וּמִבַּעַל דִּין קָשֶׁה, בֵּין שֶׁהוּא בֶן בְּרִית, וּבֵין שֶׁאֵינוֹ בֶן בְּרִית.

בָּרוּךְ שֶׁאָמַר / *Baruch She'amar*

We stand while saying the following prayer. We hold our front two tzitzis and kiss them at the end of the prayer.
This is a blessing introducing our praises of Hashem.

בָּרוּךְ שֶׁאָמַר וְהָיָה הָעוֹלָם, בָּרוּךְ הוּא. בָּרוּךְ עֹשֶׂה בְרֵאשִׁית, בָּרוּךְ אוֹמֵר וְעֹשֶׂה, בָּרוּךְ גּוֹזֵר וּמְקַיֵּם, בָּרוּךְ מְרַחֵם עַל הָאָרֶץ, בָּרוּךְ מְרַחֵם עַל הַבְּרִיּוֹת, בָּרוּךְ מְשַׁלֵּם שָׂכָר טוֹב לִירֵאָיו, בָּרוּךְ חַי לָעַד וְקַיָּם לָנֶצַח, בָּרוּךְ פּוֹדֶה וּמַצִּיל, בָּרוּךְ שְׁמוֹ. בָּרוּךְ אַתָּה יהוה אֱלֹהֵינוּ מֶלֶךְ הָעוֹלָם, הָאֵל הָאָב הָרַחֲמָן הַמְהֻלָּל בְּפֶה עַמּוֹ, מְשֻׁבָּח וּמְפֹאָר בִּלְשׁוֹן חֲסִידָיו וַעֲבָדָיו, וּבְשִׁירֵי דָוִד עַבְדֶּךָ. נְהַלֶּלְךָ יהוה אֱלֹהֵינוּ בִּשְׁבָחוֹת וּבִזְמִרוֹת, נְגַדֶּלְךָ וּנְשַׁבֵּחֲךָ וּנְפָאֶרְךָ וְנַזְכִּיר שִׁמְךָ, וְנַמְלִיכְךָ, מַלְכֵּנוּ אֱלֹהֵינוּ. יָחִיד, חֵי הָעוֹלָמִים, מֶלֶךְ מְשֻׁבָּח וּמְפֹאָר עֲדֵי עַד שְׁמוֹ הַגָּדוֹל. בָּרוּךְ אַתָּה יהוה, מֶלֶךְ מְהֻלָּל בַּתִּשְׁבָּחוֹת.

Blessed is Hashem, Who spoke, and then the whole world was created.

Blessed is Hashem, Who keeps the whole world going.

Blessed is Hashem, Who does what He says He will do.

Blessed is Hashem, Who has mercy on all that He has created.

Blessed is Hashem, Who rewards the people who fear Him.

Blessed is Hashem, Who lives forever.

Blessed is Hashem, Who saves us.

Blessed are You, Hashem, our God, King of the universe, our kind Father, Who is praised by His people through the psalms of Your servant King David. We shall praise You, Hashem, with songs and praises. We praise You, and mention Your Name, and explain to everyone how You are our King. You are the One Who gives life to the world, whose great Name is praised forever. Blessed are You, Hashem, the King Who is praised.

Did You Know??
There is a tradition that this prayer, *Baruch She'amar,* fell from Heaven on a sheet of parchment.

A Closer Look
Why is it so important for us to praise Hashem? Because when we praise Him, we come closer to Him.

אַשְׁרֵי / *Ashrei*

Whoever says *Ashrei* properly three times a day, every day,
is guaranteed a place in the World to Come.

Happy are the people
who come to shul;
they should always be able to praise You.
Happy is the nation
that is able to do this.
Happy is the nation
whose God is Hashem.

This is a song of praise,
written by King David:

א I will bless Your Name forever.

ב Every day I will praise Your Name.

ג Hashem is so great, we cannot
understand just how great He is.

ד Every generation will praise
what You do.

ה I will tell all about Your strength
and wonderful deeds.

ו They will speak about Your power,
and I will tell about Your greatness.

ז They will remember and sing
about Your goodness.

ח Hashem has mercy;
He is slow to get angry
and is very kind.

ט Hashem is good to everything
and so full of mercy;

י Everything in the world
will thank and bless You.

כ They will talk about Your glory
and Your power.

ל They will let others know
about Your might
and Your Kingship.

מ Your kingdom is forever,
in all generations.

ס Hashem supports all those
who need help.

אַשְׁרֵי יוֹשְׁבֵי בֵיתֶךָ, עוֹד יְהַלְלוּךָ סֶּלָה.
אַשְׁרֵי הָעָם שֶׁכָּכָה לּוֹ,
אַשְׁרֵי הָעָם שֶׁיהוה אֱלֹהָיו.
תְּהִלָּה לְדָוִד,
אֲרוֹמִמְךָ אֱלוֹהַי הַמֶּלֶךְ,
וַאֲבָרְכָה שִׁמְךָ לְעוֹלָם וָעֶד.
בְּכָל יוֹם אֲבָרְכֶךָּ,
וַאֲהַלְלָה שִׁמְךָ לְעוֹלָם וָעֶד.
גָּדוֹל יהוה וּמְהֻלָּל מְאֹד,
וְלִגְדֻלָּתוֹ אֵין חֵקֶר.
דּוֹר לְדוֹר יְשַׁבַּח מַעֲשֶׂיךָ, וּגְבוּרֹתֶיךָ יַגִּידוּ.
הֲדַר כְּבוֹד הוֹדֶךָ,
וְדִבְרֵי נִפְלְאֹתֶיךָ אָשִׂיחָה.
וֶעֱזוּז נוֹרְאוֹתֶיךָ יֹאמֵרוּ,
וּגְדוּלָּתְךָ אֲסַפְּרֶנָּה.
זֵכֶר רַב טוּבְךָ יַבִּיעוּ, וְצִדְקָתְךָ יְרַנֵּנוּ.
חַנּוּן וְרַחוּם יהוה,
אֶרֶךְ אַפַּיִם וּגְדָל חָסֶד.
טוֹב יהוה לַכֹּל, וְרַחֲמָיו עַל כָּל מַעֲשָׂיו.
יוֹדוּךָ יהוה כָּל מַעֲשֶׂיךָ,
וַחֲסִידֶיךָ יְבָרְכוּכָה.
כְּבוֹד מַלְכוּתְךָ יֹאמֵרוּ,
וּגְבוּרָתְךָ יְדַבֵּרוּ.
לְהוֹדִיעַ לִבְנֵי הָאָדָם גְּבוּרֹתָיו,
וּכְבוֹד הֲדַר מַלְכוּתוֹ.
מַלְכוּתְךָ מַלְכוּת כָּל עֹלָמִים,
וּמֶמְשַׁלְתְּךָ בְּכָל דּוֹר וָדֹר.
סוֹמֵךְ יהוה לְכָל הַנֹּפְלִים,
וְזוֹקֵף לְכָל הַכְּפוּפִים.

ע Everyone looks to You with hope,
and You give them their food
in its right time.

עֵינֵי כֹל אֵלֶיךָ יְשַׂבֵּרוּ,
וְאַתָּה נוֹתֵן לָהֶם אֶת אָכְלָם בְּעִתּוֹ.

23

פ Hashem, You "open" Your Hand,
and fulfill the desire of every living thing.

צ Hashem is righteous and generous.

ק Hashem is close to everyone
who calls to Him.

ר If someone fears Him,
Hashem does what they ask.

ש Hashem will protect whoever loves Him,
and destroy whoever is wicked.

ת I will say the praises of Hashem.
May everyone bless
His holy Name forever.

We will all bless God
from now and forever.

פּוֹתֵחַ אֶת יָדֶךָ, וּמַשְׂבִּיעַ לְכָל חַי רָצוֹן.

צַדִּיק יהוה בְּכָל דְּרָכָיו, וְחָסִיד בְּכָל מַעֲשָׂיו.

קָרוֹב יהוה לְכָל קֹרְאָיו,

לְכֹל אֲשֶׁר יִקְרָאֻהוּ בֶאֱמֶת.

רְצוֹן יְרֵאָיו יַעֲשֶׂה,

וְאֶת שַׁוְעָתָם יִשְׁמַע וְיוֹשִׁיעֵם.

שׁוֹמֵר יהוה אֶת כָּל אֹהֲבָיו,

וְאֵת כָּל הָרְשָׁעִים יַשְׁמִיד.

תְּהִלַּת יהוה יְדַבֶּר פִּי,

וִיבָרֵךְ כָּל בָּשָׂר שֵׁם קָדְשׁוֹ לְעוֹלָם וָעֶד.

וַאֲנַחְנוּ נְבָרֵךְ יָהּ, מֵעַתָּה וְעַד עוֹלָם, הַלְלוּיָהּ.

Did You Know??
The verse פּוֹתֵחַ praises Hashem for giving every living thing whatever it needs. That is why it is especially important to concentrate on the meaning of each word as it is being said.

24

יִשְׁתַּבַּח / *Yishtabach*

We stand while saying the following prayer.

May Your Name be praised forever, our King. You are God, the great and holy King, in the Heavens and on the earth. Hashem, our God and the God of our fathers, it is right that we speak about You with song and praise, Hallel and music; we speak about Your power and Your rule; Your victory, Your greatness, and Your strength; Your praise and glory; Your holiness and kingship; we give You blessings and thanksgiving, from now and forever.

Blessed are You, Hashem, God, King, great in praises, God to Whom we owe our thanks. Master of miracles, Who chooses to be praised with musical songs — King, God, Who gives life to all the worlds.

יִשְׁתַּבַּח שִׁמְךָ לָעַד מַלְכֵּנוּ, הָאֵל הַמֶּלֶךְ הַגָּדוֹל וְהַקָּדוֹשׁ, בַּשָּׁמַיִם וּבָאָרֶץ. כִּי לְךָ נָאֶה, יהוה אֱלֹהֵינוּ וֵאלֹהֵי אֲבוֹתֵינוּ, שִׁיר וּשְׁבָחָה, הַלֵּל וְזִמְרָה, עֹז וּמֶמְשָׁלָה, נֶצַח, גְּדֻלָּה וּגְבוּרָה, תְּהִלָּה וְתִפְאֶרֶת, קְדֻשָּׁה וּמַלְכוּת, בְּרָכוֹת וְהוֹדָאוֹת מֵעַתָּה וְעַד עוֹלָם.

בָּרוּךְ אַתָּה יהוה, אֵל מֶלֶךְ גָּדוֹל בַּתִּשְׁבָּחוֹת, אֵל הַהוֹדָאוֹת, אֲדוֹן הַנִּפְלָאוֹת, הַבּוֹחֵר בְּשִׁירֵי זִמְרָה, מֶלֶךְ, אֵל, חֵי הָעוֹלָמִים.

Did You Know??
There are fifteen words of praise in the first half of this prayer. This reminds us of the fifteen שִׁיר הַמַּעֲלוֹת songs of praise written by King David, and the fifteen steps which went from the *Ezras Nashim* to the gate of the *Ezras Yisrael* of the *Beis HaMikdash*.

A Closer Look
Our soul is always trying to be close to Hashem. We let our soul reach out to Hashem by praying to Him.

The more we pray, the closer we get to Hashem.

בָּרְכוּ / Barchu

Barchu is said only when there is a *minyan*. The *chazzan* says:

בָּרְכוּ אֶת יהוה הַמְבֹרָךְ.

Bless Hashem, the One Who is blessed.

The people answer (and then the *chazzan* also says afterwards):

בָּרוּךְ יהוה הַמְבֹרָךְ לְעוֹלָם וָעֶד.

Blessed is Hashem, forever and ever.

Did You Know??
When Avraham tried to save the people of Sedom, Hashem agreed that if there were ten righteous people in the city, He would not destroy it. Why ten? Because ten is the smallest number of men you need to form a special group called a *minyan*.

A Closer Look
When we pray together with a *minyan*, we have the combined power of all the Jewish people together. This helps our prayers to be accepted.

שְׁמַע / *Shema*

Before we begin saying the *Shema,* we must first understand that we are doing the mitzvah of saying *Shema,* and that Hashem is our King. It is very important to say each word clearly. Boys hold their *tzitzis* with the left hand, between the pinky and the next finger. We cover our eyes with our right hand. When we pray without a *minyan* we add the first three words:

אֵל מֶלֶךְ נֶאֱמָן.

God, trustworthy King.

שְׁמַע יִשְׂרָאֵל, יהוה אֱלֹהֵינוּ, יהוה אֶחָד:

Hear, O Israel, Hashem is our God, Hashem is the only One.

We then say these words quietly:

בָּרוּךְ שֵׁם כְּבוֹד מַלְכוּתוֹ לְעוֹלָם וָעֶד.

Blessed is the Name of His wonderful kingdom forever and ever.

Did You Know??
It is a Torah commandment to recite the *Shema.* By reciting the *Shema* we are saying that Hashem is the only true God, and we accept Him as our King.

A Closer Look
Two letters in the first sentence of *Shema* are larger than the others: the ע and the ד. When you put these letters together, they spell עֵד, which means witness. This means that when we say the שְׁמַע we are witnesses telling the whole world that Hashem is the only true God.

You shall love Hashem, your God, with your whole heart, with your whole soul, and with everything you own.

These things that I command you to-day shall always be in your heart.

You shall teach them to your children.

You should speak about them while you are sitting in your home, while you are walking in the street, when you go to sleep, and when you wake up.

Tie them as a sign upon your arm and let them be between your eyes.

Write them on the doorposts of your house and on your gates.

וְאָהַבְתָּ אֵת יהוה ׀ אֱלֹהֶיךָ, בְּכָל־לְבָבְךָ, וּבְכָל־נַפְשְׁךָ, וּבְכָל־מְאֹדֶךָ: וְהָיוּ הַדְּבָרִים הָאֵלֶּה, אֲשֶׁר ׀ אָנֹכִי מְצַוְּךָ הַיּוֹם, עַל־לְבָבֶךָ: וְשִׁנַּנְתָּם לְבָנֶיךָ, וְדִבַּרְתָּ בָּם, בְּשִׁבְתְּךָ בְּבֵיתֶךָ, וּבְלֶכְתְּךָ בַדֶּרֶךְ וּבְשָׁכְבְּךָ וּבְקוּמֶךָ: וּקְשַׁרְתָּם לְאוֹת ׀ עַל־יָדֶךָ, וְהָיוּ לְטֹטָפֹת בֵּין ׀ עֵינֶיךָ: וּכְתַבְתָּם ׀ עַל־מְזֻזוֹת בֵּיתֶךָ, וּבִשְׁעָרֶיךָ:

Did You Know??
The last two verses teach us that we must put on *tefillin* every day, and that we must place *mezuzahs* on every doorpost of our house. The words of the *Shema* are written on parchment that is put inside the *tefillin* and inside the *mezuzah*.

When we say this second paragraph of the *Shema* we think about obeying all of Hashem's mitzvos. We also must think that if we do what the Torah says, Hashem will reward us. And if we do not obey the Torah, we may be punished.

And if you listen to My mitzvos that I am commanding you today, to love Hashem, your God, and to do what He wants, with your whole heart and your whole soul — then I will make sure there is the right amount of rain for the land (not too much and not too little), at the right time.

Then, you will be able to gather your grain, your wine, and your oil.

I will put grass in the fields for your cattle, and you will have food to eat and be satisfied.

But be careful, and do not serve other gods and bow down to them.

If you do that, Hashem will become angry at you and He will hold back the rain from the heavens, and nothing will grow from the ground.

And you will be sent from the holy land

וְהָיָה, אִם־שָׁמֹעַ תִּשְׁמְעוּ אֶל־מִצְוֹתַי, אֲשֶׁר ‏|‏ אָנֹכִי מְצַוֶּה ‏|‏ אֶתְכֶם הַיּוֹם, לְאַהֲבָה אֶת־יהוה ‏|‏ אֱלֹהֵיכֶם וּלְעָבְדוֹ, בְּכָל־לְבַבְכֶם, וּבְכָל־נַפְשְׁכֶם. וְנָתַתִּי מְטַר־אַרְצְכֶם בְּעִתּוֹ, יוֹרֶה וּמַלְקוֹשׁ, וְאָסַפְתָּ דְגָנֶךָ וְתִירֹשְׁךָ וְיִצְהָרֶךָ. וְנָתַתִּי ‏|‏ עֵשֶׂב ‏|‏ בְּשָׂדְךָ לִבְהֶמְתֶּךָ, וְאָכַלְתָּ וְשָׂבָעְתָּ. הִשָּׁמְרוּ לָכֶם, פֶּן־יִפְתֶּה לְבַבְכֶם, וְסַרְתֶּם וַעֲבַדְתֶּם ‏|‏ אֱלֹהִים ‏|‏ אֲחֵרִים, וְהִשְׁתַּחֲוִיתֶם לָהֶם. וְחָרָה ‏|‏ אַף־יהוה בָּכֶם, וְעָצַר ‏|‏ אֶת־הַשָּׁמַיִם, וְלֹא־יִהְיֶה מָטָר, וְהָאֲדָמָה לֹא תִתֵּן אֶת־יְבוּלָהּ, וַאֲבַדְתֶּם ‏|‏ מְהֵרָה ‏|‏ מֵעַל הָאָרֶץ הַטֹּבָה ‏|‏

that Hashem gives you.

Place these words on your heart and upon your soul.

Tie them as a sign upon your arm and let them be between your eyes.

Teach them to your children to speak about them, while you are sitting in your home, walking in the street, going to sleep, and when you wake up.

Write them on the doorposts of your house and on your gates.

This way you and your children will live a long life in the land that Hashem has promised to your parents, to have as long as there is heaven and earth.

אֲשֶׁר ׀ יְהוָה נֹתֵן לָכֶם. וְשַׂמְתֶּם ׀ אֶת־דְּבָרַי ׀ אֵלֶּה, עַל־לְבַבְכֶם וְעַל־נַפְשְׁכֶם, וּקְשַׁרְתֶּם ׀ אֹתָם לְאוֹת ׀ עַל־יֶדְכֶם, וְהָיוּ לְטוֹטָפֹת בֵּין ׀ עֵינֵיכֶם. וְלִמַּדְתֶּם ׀ אֹתָם ׀ אֶת־בְּנֵיכֶם, לְדַבֵּר בָּם, בְּשִׁבְתְּךָ בְּבֵיתֶךָ, וּבְלֶכְתְּךָ בַדֶּרֶךְ, וּבְשָׁכְבְּךָ וּבְקוּמֶךָ. וּכְתַבְתָּם ׀ עַל־מְזוּזוֹת בֵּיתֶךָ, וּבִשְׁעָרֶיךָ. לְמַעַן ׀ יִרְבּוּ ׀ יְמֵיכֶם וִימֵי בְנֵיכֶם, עַל הָאֲדָמָה ׀ אֲשֶׁר נִשְׁבַּע ׀ יְהוָה ׀ לַאֲבֹתֵיכֶם לָתֵת לָהֶם, כִּימֵי הַשָּׁמַיִם ׀ עַל־הָאָרֶץ.

Did You Know??
Rabbi Akiva was killed by the Romans for teaching Torah. The last words he said as he was being tortured by them were those of the *Shema*. He told his students, "I always hoped that I would not be afraid to give up my life for Hashem. Now that I am able to do so, I am happy."

A Closer Look
This paragraph teaches us that if we follow the laws of Hashem we will be rewarded and live happy lives in the land of Israel. If we don't follow Hashem's mitzvos, then we will be punished and sent out of the land.

When boys say this third paragraph they take the *tzitzis* and hold them in both hands.
They kiss the *tzitzis* each time they say the word "*tzitzis*," and also at the end of the paragraph,
at the word אֱמֶת. They hold the *tzitzis* to their eyes when saying וּרְאִיתֶם אֹתוֹ.

וַיֹּאמֶר ׀ יהוה ׀ אֶל־מֹשֶׁה לֵּאמֹר. דַּבֵּר ׀ אֶל־בְּנֵי ׀ יִשְׂרָאֵל, וְאָמַרְתָּ אֲלֵהֶם, וְעָשׂוּ לָהֶם צִיצִת, עַל־כַּנְפֵי בִגְדֵיהֶם לְדֹרֹתָם, וְנָתְנוּ ׀ עַל־צִיצִת הַכָּנָף, פְּתִיל תְּכֵלֶת. וְהָיָה לָכֶם לְצִיצִת, וּרְאִיתֶם ׀ אֹתוֹ, וּזְכַרְתֶּם ׀ אֶת־כָּל־מִצְוֹת ׀ יהוה, וַעֲשִׂיתֶם ׀ אֹתָם, וְלֹא תָתוּרוּ ׀ אַחֲרֵי לְבַבְכֶם וְאַחֲרֵי ׀ עֵינֵיכֶם, אֲשֶׁר־אַתֶּם זֹנִים ׀ אַחֲרֵיהֶם. לְמַעַן תִּזְכְּרוּ, וַעֲשִׂיתֶם ׀ אֶת־כָּל־מִצְוֹתָי, וִהְיִיתֶם קְדֹשִׁים לֵאלֹהֵיכֶם. אֲנִי יהוה ׀ אֱלֹהֵיכֶם, אֲשֶׁר הוֹצֵאתִי ׀ אֶתְכֶם ׀ מֵאֶרֶץ מִצְרַיִם, לִהְיוֹת לָכֶם לֵאלֹהִים, אֲנִי ׀ יהוה ׀ אֱלֹהֵיכֶם. אֱמֶת —

And Hashem said to Moshe: Speak to the Children of Israel and tell them that they must make *tzitzis* on the four corners of their clothes.

And on each group of *tzitzis* they shall add a thread of *techeiles*.

This will be your *tzitzis*.

You will see the *tzitzis* and remember all the mitzvos that Hashem commanded you and you will fulfill them. Don't go running after bad things that you may want.

Remember, and do all My mitzvos, and be holy to Hashem.

I am Hashem, your God, Who has taken you out of the land of Egypt to be Your God.

I am Hashem, your God — the true One.

A Closer Look

One of the 613 mitzvos is to remember, each day, that Hashem took us out of Egypt. When we say this third paragraph of the *Shema*, we are fulfilling this mitzvah.

Did You Know??

Looking at the *tzitzis* reminds us of all the other mitzvos. The *gematria* (number value) of the word צִיצִית is 600. צ = 90, י = 10, צ = 90, י = 10, and ת = 400. Together this adds up to 600. Add the 8 strings and 5 knots that are on each corner, and you get a total of 613 — the number of mitzvos in the Torah.

The blue *techeiles* symbolizes the sky and the heavens, reminding us that there is a God above.

Did You Know??

Techeiles is a sky-blue coloring taken from a small sea-animal called the *chilazon*. For many hundreds of years now, we do not know exactly what the *chilazon* is. Even if we don't have the *techeiles*, we are still required to follow all the other laws of *tzitzis*.

שְׁמוֹנֶה עֶשְׂרֵה / *Shemoneh Esrei*

The *Shemoneh Esrei* is the most important and main part of our prayers. We praise Hashem (in the first three blessings). We ask Him for all we need (in the middle thirteen blessings). We thank Him for helping us (in the last three blessings). When we say the *Shemoneh Esrei*, we are talking directly to Hashem, asking Him for everything we need and thanking Him for everything we have.

We first take three steps backwards and then three steps forward. It is as if we are coming closer to Hashem. We stand with our feet together during the entire *Shemoneh Esrei*.

At *Minchah* begin here:

כִּי שֵׁם יהוה אֶקְרָא, הָבוּ גֹדֶל לֵאלֹהֵינוּ.
When I call out the Name of Hashem, I speak greatness of our God.

My Lord, open my lips so I can praise You.
אֲדֹנָי שְׂפָתַי תִּפְתָּח, וּפִי יַגִּיד תְּהִלָּתֶךָ.

Berachah 1: אָבוֹת / FATHERS

In the first *berachah* we speak about Hashem's greatness and how He guided our forefathers.
In this *berachah* we bend our knees when we say בָּרוּךְ, and we bow when we say אַתָּה.
Then we stand up straight when we say the Name of Hashem.

Blessed are You, Hashem, our God and the God of our fathers, the God of Avraham, the God of Yitzchak, and the God of Yaakov, the mighty, powerful, and supreme God; Who is kind, and owns everything, Who remembers the good deeds of our fathers, and brings the Mashiach to their children, for His sake, with love.

בָּרוּךְ אַתָּה יהוה אֱלֹהֵינוּ וֵאלֹהֵי אֲבוֹתֵינוּ, אֱלֹהֵי אַבְרָהָם, אֱלֹהֵי יִצְחָק, וֵאלֹהֵי יַעֲקֹב, הָאֵל הַגָּדוֹל הַגִּבּוֹר וְהַנּוֹרָא, אֵל עֶלְיוֹן, גּוֹמֵל חֲסָדִים טוֹבִים, וְקוֹנֵה הַכֹּל, וְזוֹכֵר חַסְדֵי אָבוֹת, וּמֵבִיא גוֹאֵל לִבְנֵי בְנֵיהֶם, לְמַעַן שְׁמוֹ בְּאַהֲבָה.

Did You Know??
Another word for prayer is "*avodah.*" *Avodah* means work. Proper prayer is real work; we must work hard to pray properly. That means we should try to learn what the words mean, and when we pray we should not think about other things. Some of our Sages prepared themselves for an hour before they prayed!
Shemoneh Esrei should be recited quietly in a whisper. This is because when Chanah prayed for a son, her voice was also not heard. The way Chanah spoke to Hashem is the example of how prayer should be said.

A Closer Look
When we pray, it is important that we understand before Whom we are standing. If we would be frightened standing before a king, imagine how we should feel when we are standing before Hashem, the King of kings!

Between Rosh Hashanah and Yom Kippur we add:

Remember us for life, Hashem, Who wants life.
Write us in the Book of Life — for Your sake.

זָכְרֵנוּ לְחַיִּים, מֶלֶךְ חָפֵץ בַּחַיִּים, וְכָתְבֵנוּ בְּסֵפֶר הַחַיִּים, לְמַעַנְךָ אֱלֹהִים חַיִּים.

We bend our knees when we say בָּרוּךְ, and we bow when we say אַתָּה.
Then we stand up straight when we say the Name of Hashem.

You are the King, Who saves us and helps us. Blessed are You, Hashem, the protector of Avraham.

מֶלֶךְ עוֹזֵר וּמוֹשִׁיעַ וּמָגֵן. בָּרוּךְ אַתָּה יהוה, מָגֵן אַבְרָהָם.

Berachah 2: גבורות / GOD'S POWER

In the second *berachah* we praise Hashem for His mighty deeds,
including that when Mashiach comes Hashem will bring the dead back to life.

You are powerful forever, my Lord.
You bring the dead back to life,
You are able to save.

אַתָּה גִּבּוֹר לְעוֹלָם אֲדֹנָי, מְחַיֵּה מֵתִים אַתָּה, רַב לְהוֹשִׁיעַ.

Between Shemini Atzeres and Pesach we add:

You make the wind blow and the rain fall.

מַשִּׁיב הָרוּחַ וּמוֹרִיד הַגֶּשֶׁם.

Between Pesach and Shemini Atzeres, *Nusach Sefard* and people in Eretz Yisrael add:

You make the dew fall.

מוֹרִיד הַטָּל.

You keep us alive with kindness. You bring the dead back to life. You support those who fall. You heal the sick. You free the prisoners. And You keep Your promise to the dead to bring them back to life. Who is like You, our King, Who causes people to die, and brings them back to life.

מְכַלְכֵּל חַיִּים בְּחֶסֶד, מְחַיֵּה מֵתִים בְּרַחֲמִים רַבִּים, סוֹמֵךְ נוֹפְלִים, וְרוֹפֵא חוֹלִים, וּמַתִּיר אֲסוּרִים, וּמְקַיֵּם אֱמוּנָתוֹ לִישֵׁנֵי עָפָר. מִי כָמוֹךָ בַּעַל גְּבוּרוֹת, וּמִי דוֹמֶה לָּךְ, מֶלֶךְ מֵמִית וּמְחַיֶּה וּמַצְמִיחַ יְשׁוּעָה.

Did You Know??
At first, the *Shemoneh Esrei* (which means 18) had 18 blessings. After the Second *Beis HaMikdash* was destroyed, our Sages added a 19th blessing, וְלַמַּלְשִׁינִים. This was a prayer to Hashem to protect us from all enemies of the Torah and the Jewish people.

A Closer Look
In the first blessing of the *Shemoneh Esrei*, we speak about our forefathers and ask God to bless us for their sake. Our Sages tell us that we must take special care to concentrate on the meaning of this first *berachah*.

Did You Know??
When we pray, we are like the Avos: Avraham, Yitzchak, and Yaakov. They were the first people to pray *Shacharis*, *Minchah*, and *Maariv*.

Did You Know??
When we say the *Shemoneh Esrei* we should stand with our feet together. Our Sages teach us that we should keep our feet together when praying so that we will look like angels who appear to have one straight leg.

Who is like You, Father Who is merciful,
Who remembers everyone in order that they live.

מִי כָמְוֹךְ אַב הָרַחֲמִים,
זוֹכֵר יְצוּרָיו לְחַיִּים בְּרַחֲמִים.

We trust You to bring the dead back to life.
Blessed are You, Hashem, Who brings the dead back to life.

וְנֶאֱמָן אַתָּה לְהַחֲיוֹת מֵתִים. בָּרוּךְ אַתָּה
יהוה, מְחַיֵּה הַמֵּתִים.

Berachah 3: קְדֻשַׁת הַשֵּׁם / THE HOLINESS OF HASHEM

In the third *berachah* we praise Hashem for being holy.

You are holy and Your Name is holy, and holy ones praise You every day. Blessed are You, Hashem, °the holy God.

אַתָּה קָדוֹשׁ וְשִׁמְךָ קָדוֹשׁ, וּקְדוֹשִׁים
בְּכָל יוֹם יְהַלְלוּךָ סֶּלָה. בָּרוּךְ
אַתָּה יהוה, °הָאֵל הַקָּדוֹשׁ.

Did You Know??
Nothing is greater or stronger than the power of prayer.

A Closer Look
Prayer is called "service of the heart." Prayer connects our heart directly to Hashem.

Berachah 4: דַעַת / WISDOM

In the fourth *berachah* we ask Hashem to give us wisdom.

אַתָּה חוֹנֵן לְאָדָם דַּעַת, וּמְלַמֵּד לֶאֱנוֹשׁ בִּינָה. חָנֵּנוּ מֵאִתְּךָ דֵּעָה בִּינָה וְהַשְׂכֵּל. בָּרוּךְ אַתָּה יהוה, חוֹנֵן הַדָּעַת.

You give wisdom to man and teach understanding to people. Please give us wisdom and understanding. Blessed are You, Hashem, Who gives people wisdom.

Did You Know??
This blessing begins the middle section of the *Shemoneh Esrei* where we ask God for things that we need. The first thing we ask for is wisdom. Wisdom is so important because it separates people from animals.

Berachah 5: תְּשׁוּבָה / REPENTANCE

In the fifth *berachah* we ask Hashem to help us do *teshuvah* (repentance).

הֲשִׁיבֵנוּ אָבִינוּ לְתוֹרָתֶךָ, וְקָרְבֵנוּ מַלְכֵּנוּ לַעֲבוֹדָתֶךָ, וְהַחֲזִירֵנוּ בִּתְשׁוּבָה שְׁלֵמָה לְפָנֶיךָ. בָּרוּךְ אַתָּה יהוה, הָרוֹצֶה בִּתְשׁוּבָה.

Bring us back, our Father, to Your Torah, and bring us close to You. Make us feel sorry for the bad things we did and help us do *teshuvah*. Blessed are You, Hashem, Who wants us to repent.

A Closer Look
Why can't Hashem just give us everything we need? Why must we pray to Him every day? Hashem loves to hear our prayers because when we pray and think about how we need Hashem to help us, we become better people.

Berachah 6: סְלִיחָה / FORGIVENESS

In the sixth *berachah* we ask Hashem to forgive our sins.

סְלַח לָנוּ אָבִינוּ כִּי חָטָאנוּ, מְחַל לָנוּ מַלְכֵּנוּ כִּי פָשָׁעְנוּ, כִּי מוֹחֵל וְסוֹלֵחַ אָתָּה. בָּרוּךְ אַתָּה יהוה, חַנּוּן הַמַּרְבֶּה לִסְלוֹחַ.

Forgive us, our Father, for any sins we have done. Forgive us even for the times we sinned on purpose. Blessed are You, Hashem, Who forgives our sins.

Did You Know??
In the paragraph סְלַח לָנוּ, we hit the left side of our chest, over our heart, while saying the words חָטָאנוּ (sins we have done) and פָשָׁעְנוּ (we have sinned on purpose).

Berachah 7: גְּאוּלָה / SALVATION

In the seventh *berachah* we ask Hashem to redeem us.

רְאֵה בְעָנְיֵנוּ, וְרִיבָה רִיבֵנוּ, וּגְאָלֵנוּ מְהֵרָה לְמַעַן שְׁמֶךָ, כִּי גוֹאֵל חָזָק אָתָּה. בָּרוּךְ אַתָּה יהוה, גוֹאֵל יִשְׂרָאֵל.

Look at our suffering. Help us when we have problems. Help us quickly for Your sake, for You are the great Redeemer. Blessed are You, Hashem, Redeemer of Israel.

A Closer Look
In this prayer we beg Hashem to redeem us from the troubles of everyday life. Further on, in *berachah* 10, תְּקַע בְּשׁוֹפָר, we ask Hashem to redeem the Jewish people by bringing the Mashiach.

Berachah 8: רְפוּאָה / HEALING

In the eighth *berachah* we ask Hashem to heal sick people.

רְפָאֵנוּ יהוה וְנֵרָפֵא, הוֹשִׁיעֵנוּ וְנִוָּשֵׁעָה, כִּי תְהִלָּתֵנוּ אָתָּה, וְהַעֲלֵה רְפוּאָה שְׁלֵמָה לְכָל מַכּוֹתֵינוּ,* כִּי אֵל מֶלֶךְ רוֹפֵא נֶאֱמָן וְרַחֲמָן אָתָּה. בָּרוּךְ אַתָּה יהוה, רוֹפֵא חוֹלֵי עַמּוֹ יִשְׂרָאֵל.

Heal us, Hashem, and we will be truly healed. Give us a complete recovery from all our sicknesses,* because You are God, the King Who is the merciful Healer. Blessed are You, Hashem, Who heals the sick of the people of Israel.

---

* At this point, if we want, we can add a special prayer for a particular sick person.

Did You Know??
Our Sages made the prayer for healing the 8th *berachah* of the *Shemoneh Esrei*. This reminds us to include in our prayers all the Jewish baby boys who are having their *bris milah* on the 8th day after their birth.

A Closer Look
When we pray for others to be healed, then Hashem heals us also. When we pray for others, our prayers for ourselves are answered more quickly.

Berachah 9: בִּרְכַּת הַשָּׁנִים / YEAR OF PLENTY

In the ninth *berachah* we ask Hashem to bless the crops in the ground, to give us the right amount of rain, and in general to allow us to earn a living.

בָּרֵךְ עָלֵינוּ יהוה אֱלֹהֵינוּ אֶת הַשָּׁנָה הַזֹּאת וְאֶת כָּל מִינֵי תְבוּאָתָהּ לְטוֹבָה, וְתֵן

Bless for us, Hashem, our God, this year and its crops. Give us

---

during the summer: a blessing

during the winter: dew and rain for a blessing

---

on the earth. Bless our year, and make this the best year possible. Blessed are You, Hashem, Who blesses the years.

בְּרָכָה — during the summer

טַל וּמָטָר לִבְרָכָה — during the winter

עַל פְּנֵי הָאֲדָמָה, וְשַׂבְּעֵנוּ מִטּוּבֶךָ, וּבָרֵךְ שְׁנָתֵנוּ כַּשָּׁנִים הַטּוֹבוֹת. בָּרוּךְ אַתָּה יהוה, מְבָרֵךְ הַשָּׁנִים.

Did You Know??
Wintertime (December 5th till Pesach) is the rainy season. Wherever we live, we pray that there should be enough rain so people will have enough food to eat.

A Closer Look
When we recite this blessing, we should have in mind that Hashem should give our parents everything they need to support us and our whole family.

Did You Know??
One year there was no rain in Eretz Yisrael. Rabbi Eliezer told everyone to fast 13 separate times in order that it would rain. Still, no rain came. Finally, all the people were so hungry they thought they would die. The people began praying and tears fell from their eyes. When that happened, the rain began to fall.

Berachah 10: קִבּוּץ גָּלִיּוֹת / GATHERING OF EXILES

In the tenth *berachah* we ask Hashem to gather all the Jews together in Eretz Yisrael.

Blow the great shofar for our freedom, and gather our exiles from the four corners of the earth (to Eretz Yisrael). Blessed are You, Hashem, Who gathers the nation of Israel from all over the earth.

תְּקַע בְּשׁוֹפָר גָּדוֹל לְחֵרוּתֵנוּ, וְשָׂא נֵס לְקַבֵּץ גָּלִיּוֹתֵינוּ, וְקַבְּצֵנוּ יַחַד מֵאַרְבַּע כַּנְפוֹת הָאָרֶץ. בָּרוּךְ אַתָּה יהוה, מְקַבֵּץ נִדְחֵי עַמּוֹ יִשְׂרָאֵל.

Did You Know??
In this paragraph we pray for the final redemption, when Hashem will bring the Mashiach and all the Jews will come back to Eretz Yisrael. The whole world will hear the great shofar and Eliyahu will announce the coming of Mashiach.

Berachah 11: דִּין / JUSTICE

In the eleventh *berachah* we ask Hashem to give us proper leaders and judges.

Bring back judges like we used to have, and advisers as there once were. Take away our troubles. We want You, Hashem, with Your kindness and Your mercy, to be our King and to judge us favorably with justice. Blessed are You, Hashem, °the King, Who loves righteousness and justice.

הָשִׁיבָה שׁוֹפְטֵינוּ כְּבָרִאשׁוֹנָה, וְיוֹעֲצֵינוּ כְּבַתְּחִלָּה, וְהָסֵר מִמֶּנּוּ יָגוֹן וַאֲנָחָה, וּמְלוֹךְ עָלֵינוּ אַתָּה יהוה לְבַדְּךָ בְּחֶסֶד וּבְרַחֲמִים, וְצַדְּקֵנוּ בַּמִּשְׁפָּט. בָּרוּךְ אַתָּה יהוה, °מֶלֶךְ אוֹהֵב צְדָקָה וּמִשְׁפָּט.

Between Rosh Hashanah and Yom Kippur,
instead of מֶלֶךְ אוֹהֵב צְדָקָה וּמִשְׁפָּט, *the King Who loves righteousness and justice,* we say:
°the King of justice.
°הַמֶּלֶךְ הַמִּשְׁפָּט.

Did You Know??
Our Sages teach us that no matter how bad a situation is — even if a sharp sword is already at our neck — we should not stop praying. Hashem can always make a miracle happen.

Berachah 12: בְּרְכַּת הַמִּינִים / AGAINST THE WICKED

In the twelfth *berachah* we ask Hashem to destroy our enemies.

And those who talk and act badly towards the Jewish people should be punished. May all evil be destroyed and may all Your enemies be wiped out quickly. Destroy the bad people in our days. Blessed are You, Hashem, Who destroys enemies and sinners.

A Closer Look
See the note on page 33 to see why and when this *berachah* was added.

וְלַמַּלְשִׁינִים אַל תְּהִי תִקְוָה, וְכָל הָרִשְׁעָה כְּרֶגַע תֹּאבֵד, וְכָל אוֹיְבֶיךָ מְהֵרָה יִכָּרֵתוּ, וְהַזֵּדִים מְהֵרָה תְעַקֵּר וּתְשַׁבֵּר וּתְמַגֵּר וְתַכְנִיעַ בִּמְהֵרָה בְיָמֵינוּ. בָּרוּךְ אַתָּה יהוה, שׁוֹבֵר אֹיְבִים וּמַכְנִיעַ זֵדִים.

Berachah 13: צַדִּיקִים / THE RIGHTEOUS

In the thirteenth *berachah* we ask Hashem to reward the righteous people, and to include us among the righteous.

When You deal with all types of righteous people, may You be compassionate, Hashem, our God. Give good reward to all those who believe and trust in Your Name. Include us with them, and let us not be ashamed, because we trust in You. Blessed are You, Hashem, Who supports the righteous.

Did You Know??
If our prayers are not answered the way we want, we should pray again, and again, and again.

עַל הַצַּדִּיקִים וְעַל הַחֲסִידִים, וְעַל זִקְנֵי עַמְּךָ בֵּית יִשְׂרָאֵל, וְעַל פְּלֵיטַת סוֹפְרֵיהֶם, וְעַל גֵּרֵי הַצֶּדֶק, וְעָלֵינוּ, יֶהֱמוּ רַחֲמֶיךָ, יהוה אֱלֹהֵינוּ, וְתֵן שָׂכָר טוֹב לְכָל הַבּוֹטְחִים בְּשִׁמְךָ בֶּאֱמֶת, וְשִׂים חֶלְקֵנוּ עִמָּהֶם לְעוֹלָם, וְלֹא נֵבוֹשׁ כִּי בְךָ בָּטָחְנוּ. בָּרוּךְ אַתָּה יהוה, מִשְׁעָן וּמִבְטָח לַצַּדִּיקִים.

Berachah 14: בִּנְיַן יְרוּשָׁלַיִם / REBUILDING JERUSALEM

In the fourteenth *berachah* we ask Hashem to rebuild the city of Jerusalem.

Please return to Jerusalem, Your city, with mercy and be there as You said You would. Rebuild it soon, in our time, forever. And may You establish the throne of David right away within Jerusalem. Blessed are You, Hashem, the Builder of Jerusalem.

וְלִירוּשָׁלַיִם עִירְךָ בְּרַחֲמִים תָּשׁוּב, וְתִשְׁכּוֹן בְּתוֹכָהּ כַּאֲשֶׁר דִּבַּרְתָּ, וּבְנֵה אוֹתָהּ בְּקָרוֹב בְּיָמֵינוּ בִּנְיַן עוֹלָם, וְכִסֵּא דָוִד מְהֵרָה לְתוֹכָהּ תָּכִין. בָּרוּךְ אַתָּה יהוה, בּוֹנֵה יְרוּשָׁלַיִם.

> **A Closer Look**
> For almost 2,000 years, Hashem has been with the Jewish people in exile. We pray for Hashem to return with us to Eretz Yisrael and to rebuild His holy city, Jerusalem.

Berachah 15: מַלְכוּת בֵּית דָוִד / KINGDOM OF DAVID

In the fifteenth *berachah* we ask Hashem to save us and bring back the kingdom of David HaMelech.

Bring back the Kingdom of David, and let it grow stronger and stronger. Send us Your salvation, because that is what we are waiting for. Blessed are You, Hashem, Who makes the seeds of our salvation grow.

אֶת צֶמַח דָּוִד עַבְדְּךָ מְהֵרָה תַצְמִיחַ, וְקַרְנוֹ תָּרוּם בִּישׁוּעָתֶךָ, כִּי לִישׁוּעָתְךָ קִוִּינוּ כָּל הַיּוֹם. בָּרוּךְ אַתָּה יהוה, מַצְמִיחַ קֶרֶן יְשׁוּעָה.

> **A Closer Look**
> It is only when Mashiach, the descendant of David, will come and all the Jews will be brought back to Eretz Yisrael that we will be truly redeemed.

Berachah 16: קַבָּלַת תְּפִלָּה / ACCEPTANCE OF PRAYER

In the sixteenth *berachah* we ask Hashem to accept our prayers.

Listen to our voice, Hashem, our God. Have pity on us, and accept our prayer, because You are God, Who hears our prayers. Do not turn us away empty-handed, because You hear our prayers with mercy. Blessed are You, Hashem, Who listens to prayer.

שְׁמַע קוֹלֵנוּ יהוה אֱלֹהֵינוּ, חוּס וְרַחֵם עָלֵינוּ, וְקַבֵּל בְּרַחֲמִים וּבְרָצוֹן אֶת תְּפִלָּתֵנוּ, כִּי אֵל שׁוֹמֵעַ תְּפִלּוֹת וְתַחֲנוּנִים אָתָּה. וּמִלְּפָנֶיךָ מַלְכֵּנוּ רֵיקָם אַל תְּשִׁיבֵנוּ. כִּי אַתָּה שׁוֹמֵעַ תְּפִלַּת עַמְּךָ יִשְׂרָאֵל בְּרַחֲמִים. בָּרוּךְ אַתָּה יהוה, שׁוֹמֵעַ תְּפִלָּה.

A Closer Look

Hashem hears all of our prayers, all the time.

Our Sages teach us that the Gates of Tears are always open. Whenever a person cries from his heart, his prayers are listened to.

The final section of *Shemoneh Esrei* begins here.
We thank Hashem for listening to our prayers and hearing what we had to say.

Berachah 17: עֲבוֹדָה / TEMPLE SERVICE

In the seventeenth *berachah* we pray for Hashem's Presence to return to Eretz Yisrael.

Act kindly, Hashem, our God, toward Your people Israel and to their prayer. Bring back the Temple service to the *Beis HaMikdash*. Accept their offerings and prayers with love and desire. And may You always want to accept the service of Your people Israel.

רְצֵה יהוה אֱלֹהֵינוּ בְּעַמְּךָ יִשְׂרָאֵל וּבִתְפִלָּתָם, וְהָשֵׁב אֶת הָעֲבוֹדָה לִדְבִיר בֵּיתֶךָ וְאִשֵּׁי יִשְׂרָאֵל. וּתְפִלָּתָם בְּאַהֲבָה תְקַבֵּל בְּרָצוֹן, וּתְהִי לְרָצוֹן תָּמִיד עֲבוֹדַת יִשְׂרָאֵל עַמֶּךָ.

Did You Know??

Our prayers today take the place of the sacrifices that were offered in the *Beis HaMikdash*. Just as the sacrifices then had to be without blemishes, so should our prayers be without mistakes or bad thoughts.

יַעֲלֶה וְיָבֹא / Yaaleh V'yavo

On Rosh Chodesh and Chol HaMoed add the following paragraph:

אֱלֹהֵינוּ וֵאלֹהֵי אֲבוֹתֵינוּ, יַעֲלֶה, וְיָבֹא, וְיַגִּיעַ, וְיֵרָאֶה, וְיֵרָצֶה, וְיִשָּׁמַע, וְיִפָּקֵד, וְיִזָּכֵר, זִכְרוֹנֵנוּ וּפִקְדוֹנֵנוּ, וְזִכְרוֹן אֲבוֹתֵינוּ, וְזִכְרוֹן מָשִׁיחַ בֶּן דָּוִד עַבְדֶּךָ, וְזִכְרוֹן יְרוּשָׁלַיִם עִיר קָדְשֶׁךָ, וְזִכְרוֹן כָּל עַמְּךָ בֵּית יִשְׂרָאֵל לְפָנֶיךָ, לִפְלֵיטָה לְטוֹבָה לְחֵן וּלְחֶסֶד וּלְרַחֲמִים, לְחַיִּים וּלְשָׁלוֹם, בְּיוֹם

on Rosh Chodesh say: — רֹאשׁ הַחֹדֶשׁ הַזֶּה.

on Pesach say: — חַג הַמַּצּוֹת הַזֶּה.

on Succos say: — חַג הַסֻּכּוֹת הַזֶּה.

זָכְרֵנוּ יהוה אֱלֹהֵינוּ בּוֹ לְטוֹבָה, וּפָקְדֵנוּ בוֹ לִבְרָכָה, וְהוֹשִׁיעֵנוּ בוֹ לְחַיִּים. וּבִדְבַר יְשׁוּעָה וְרַחֲמִים, חוּס וְחָנֵּנוּ וְרַחֵם עָלֵינוּ וְהוֹשִׁיעֵנוּ, כִּי אֵלֶיךָ עֵינֵינוּ, כִּי אֵל (מֶלֶךְ) חַנּוּן וְרַחוּם אָתָּה.

Our God and God of our fathers, we pray that the following thoughts will be heard and recalled by You: memories of us; of our fathers; of Mashiach, from the family of David; of Jerusalem, Your holy city; and of the entire nation of Israel.

Remember all these to rescue us, to give us goodness, love, and kindness, life and peace, on this day of

on Rosh Chodesh say: Rosh Chodesh,

on Pesach say: the Festival of Matzos,

on Succos say: the Succos Festival.

Remember us, Hashem, our God, for good, for blessing, and for life. Have pity on us and save us, because we look to You for help, since You are the generous God, filled with mercy.

A Closer Look

In יַעֲלֶה וְיָבֹא we ask Hashem to remember us for good things, as He did in the days of old when we brought special offerings on Rosh Chodesh and the holidays.

May our eyes see You return to Eretz Yisrael with mercy. Blessed are You, Hashem, Who brings His Presence back to Eretz Yisrael.

וְתֶחֱזֶינָה עֵינֵינוּ בְּשׁוּבְךָ לְצִיּוֹן בְּרַחֲמִים. בָּרוּךְ אַתָּה יהוה, הַמַּחֲזִיר שְׁכִינָתוֹ לְצִיּוֹן.

Berachah 18: הוֹדָאָה / THANKSGIVING

In the eighteenth *berachah* we give thanks to Hashem for all He does for us.
We bow when we say מוֹדִים and we straighten up when we say ה'.

We thank You, because You are Hashem, our God and the God of our fathers, forever. You are our strength from generation to generation. We thank You and praise You. Our lives are in Your hands; our souls are dedicated to You. Your miracles are with us every day; Your good deeds are with us all the time; in the evening, in the morning, and in the afternoon. You are the Good One, and You are always filled with compassion. You are the Merciful One, and Your kindness is forever. We always put our hope in You.

מוֹדִים אֲנַחְנוּ לָךְ שָׁאַתָּה הוּא יהוה אֱלֹהֵינוּ וֵאלֹהֵי אֲבוֹתֵינוּ לְעוֹלָם וָעֶד. צוּר חַיֵּינוּ, מָגֵן יִשְׁעֵנוּ אַתָּה הוּא לְדוֹר וָדוֹר. נוֹדֶה לְּךָ וּנְסַפֵּר תְּהִלָּתֶךָ עַל חַיֵּינוּ הַמְּסוּרִים בְּיָדֶךָ, וְעַל נִשְׁמוֹתֵינוּ הַפְּקוּדוֹת לָךְ, וְעַל נִסֶּיךָ שֶׁבְּכָל יוֹם עִמָּנוּ, וְעַל נִפְלְאוֹתֶיךָ וְטוֹבוֹתֶיךָ שֶׁבְּכָל עֵת, עֶרֶב וָבֹקֶר וְצָהֳרָיִם. הַטּוֹב כִּי לֹא כָלוּ רַחֲמֶיךָ, וְהַמְרַחֵם כִּי לֹא תַמּוּ חֲסָדֶיךָ, מֵעוֹלָם קִוִּינוּ לָךְ.

A Closer Look
When we thank Hashem we realize that without His help we cannot do anything. Without Him, we would not even be alive.

We must praise Hashem when things are good and we must also praise Hashem when things look bad.

עַל הַנִּסִּים / Al HaNissim

On Chanukah and Purim we add the following:

(וְ)עַל הַנִּסִּים, וְעַל הַפֻּרְקָן, וְעַל הַגְּבוּרוֹת, וְעַל הַתְּשׁוּעוֹת, וְעַל הַמִּלְחָמוֹת, שֶׁעָשִׂיתָ לַאֲבוֹתֵינוּ בַּיָּמִים הָהֵם בַּזְּמַן הַזֶּה.

And (we thank Hashem) for the miracles, and for saving us, and for the victories in the wars, which You did for our fathers, in those days, in this time of the year.

A Closer Look

Our enemies knew that if they wanted to destroy the Jewish people they must not let us follow Hashem's laws, and not let us learn His Torah. But in truth, this can never happen, and the Jewish people will never be destroyed. This was Hashem's promise to our father Avraham.

בִּימֵי מַתִּתְיָהוּ בֶּן יוֹחָנָן כֹּהֵן גָּדוֹל חַשְׁמוֹנָאִי וּבָנָיו, כְּשֶׁעָמְדָה מַלְכוּת יָוָן הָרְשָׁעָה עַל עַמְּךָ יִשְׂרָאֵל, לְהַשְׁכִּיחָם תּוֹרָתֶךָ, וּלְהַעֲבִירָם מֵחֻקֵּי רְצוֹנֶךָ. וְאַתָּה בְּרַחֲמֶיךָ הָרַבִּים, עָמַדְתָּ לָהֶם בְּעֵת צָרָתָם, רַבְתָּ אֶת רִיבָם, דַּנְתָּ אֶת דִּינָם, נָקַמְתָּ אֶת נִקְמָתָם. מָסַרְתָּ גִבּוֹרִים בְּיַד חַלָּשִׁים, וְרַבִּים בְּיַד מְעַטִּים, וּטְמֵאִים בְּיַד טְהוֹרִים, וּרְשָׁעִים בְּיַד צַדִּיקִים, וְזֵדִים בְּיַד עוֹסְקֵי תוֹרָתֶךָ. וּלְךָ עָשִׂיתָ שֵׁם גָּדוֹל וְקָדוֹשׁ בְּעוֹלָמֶךָ, וּלְעַמְּךָ יִשְׂרָאֵל עָשִׂיתָ תְּשׁוּעָה גְדוֹלָה וּפֻרְקָן כְּהַיּוֹם הַזֶּה. וְאַחַר כֵּן בָּאוּ בָנֶיךָ לִדְבִיר בֵּיתֶךָ, וּפִנּוּ אֶת הֵיכָלֶךָ, וְטִהֲרוּ אֶת מִקְדָּשֶׁךָ, וְהִדְלִיקוּ נֵרוֹת בְּחַצְרוֹת קָדְשֶׁךָ, וְקָבְעוּ שְׁמוֹנַת יְמֵי חֲנֻכָּה אֵלּוּ, לְהוֹדוֹת וּלְהַלֵּל לְשִׁמְךָ הַגָּדוֹל.

In the days of Mattisyahu the son of Yochanan the Kohen, the Chashmonean, and his sons. The evil Greek kingdom stood against Your nation, and tried to make them forget Your Torah, and tried to force them not to follow Your laws.

And You, with Your great mercy, stood up for the Jews in their time of suffering. You listened to them and took revenge for them. You gave the strong (Greeks) into the hands of the weak (Jewish people); the many into the hands of the few; the impure into the hands of the pure; the wicked ones into the hands of the *tzaddikim*; and the evil ones into the hands of the ones who study Your Torah. You made Your Name great and holy in Your world. And as for Your nation, Israel, You made for them a great victory and a salvation which lasts until today. Afterwards, Your children came to Your *Beis HaMikdash* and to the Holy of Holies, purified Your Temple, and lit the lamps in the yard of Your Holy Place. And they established these eight days of Chanukah, in order to give thanks and to praise Your great Name.

בִּימֵי מָרְדְּכַי וְאֶסְתֵּר בְּשׁוּשַׁן הַבִּירָה, כְּשֶׁעָמַד עֲלֵיהֶם הָמָן הָרָשָׁע, בִּקֵּשׁ לְהַשְׁמִיד לַהֲרֹג וּלְאַבֵּד אֶת כָּל הַיְּהוּדִים, מִנַּעַר וְעַד זָקֵן, טַף וְנָשִׁים בְּיוֹם אֶחָד, בִּשְׁלֹשָׁה עָשָׂר לְחֹדֶשׁ שְׁנֵים עָשָׂר, הוּא חֹדֶשׁ אֲדָר, וּשְׁלָלָם לָבוֹז. וְאַתָּה בְּרַחֲמֶיךָ הָרַבִּים הֵפַרְתָּ אֶת עֲצָתוֹ, וְקִלְקַלְתָּ אֶת מַחֲשַׁבְתּוֹ, וַהֲשֵׁבוֹתָ לּוֹ גְמוּלוֹ בְּרֹאשׁוֹ, וְתָלוּ אוֹתוֹ וְאֶת בָּנָיו עַל הָעֵץ.

In the days of Mordechai and Esther in the capital city of Shushan, the evil Haman stood up against the Jews and tried to destroy them. He wanted to kill all the Jews, young and old, babies and women, all on the same day, on the thirteenth day of Adar, the twelfth month, and steal all they owned.

But You, with mercy, stopped him and caused everything he wanted to do to the Jewish people to happen to him instead. And so they hanged Haman and his sons from the tree.

And for all those things that You do, may Your Name be blessed forever.

וְעַל כֻּלָּם יִתְבָּרַךְ וְיִתְרוֹמַם שִׁמְךָ מַלְכֵּנוּ תָּמִיד לְעוֹלָם וָעֶד.

Between Rosh Hashanah and Yom Kippur we add:

And write down all Jews, the children of Your covenant, for a good life.

וּכְתוֹב לְחַיִּים טוֹבִים כָּל בְּנֵי בְרִיתֶךָ.

We bend our knees when we say בָּרוּךְ, and we bow when we say אַתָּה.
Then we stand up straight when we say the Name of Hashem.

May everything alive thank You, and praise Your Name, because Hashem saves us and helps us. Blessed are You, Hashem, Your Name is "The Good One" and it is proper to give thanks to You.

וְכֹל הַחַיִּים יוֹדוּךָ סֶּלָה, וִיהַלְלוּ אֶת שִׁמְךָ בֶּאֱמֶת. הָאֵל יְשׁוּעָתֵנוּ וְעֶזְרָתֵנוּ סֶלָה. בָּרוּךְ אַתָּה יהוה, הַטּוֹב שִׁמְךָ וּלְךָ נָאֶה לְהוֹדוֹת.

Berachah 19: שָׁלוֹם / PEACE

In the nineteenth and final *berachah* we ask Hashem for peace in the world.

Place peace, goodness, blessing, kindness and mercy on us and upon all Your nation, Israel. Bless us, our Father, with Your light. It is through Your light, Hashem, our God, that You have given us the Torah which gives Life. And You give us a love of kindness, charity, blessing, compassion, life and peace. And it should be proper in Your eyes to bless Your people, Israel, all the time, with peace.°

שִׂים שָׁלוֹם, טוֹבָה, וּבְרָכָה, חֵן, וָחֶסֶד וְרַחֲמִים, עָלֵינוּ וְעַל כָּל יִשְׂרָאֵל עַמֶּךָ. בָּרְכֵנוּ אָבִינוּ, כֻּלָּנוּ כְּאֶחָד בְּאוֹר פָּנֶיךָ, כִּי בְאוֹר פָּנֶיךָ נָתַתָּ לָּנוּ, יהוה אֱלֹהֵינוּ, תּוֹרַת חַיִּים וְאַהֲבַת חֶסֶד, וּצְדָקָה, וּבְרָכָה, וְרַחֲמִים, וְחַיִּים, וְשָׁלוֹם. וְטוֹב בְּעֵינֶיךָ לְבָרֵךְ אֶת עַמְּךָ יִשְׂרָאֵל, בְּכָל עֵת וּבְכָל שָׁעָה בִּשְׁלוֹמֶךָ.°

°Between Rosh Hashanah and Yom Kippur we add:

In the book of life, blessing, peace, and livelihood may You remember us and write us, and Your whole nation, the Jewish people, for a good and peaceful life.

בְּסֵפֶר חַיִּים בְּרָכָה וְשָׁלוֹם, וּפַרְנָסָה טוֹבָה, נִזָּכֵר וְנִכָּתֵב לְפָנֶיךָ, אֲנַחְנוּ וְכָל עַמְּךָ בֵּית יִשְׂרָאֵל, לְחַיִּים טוֹבִים וּלְשָׁלוֹם.

Blessed are You, Hashem, Who blesses His people, Israel, with peace.

בָּרוּךְ אַתָּה יהוה, הַמְבָרֵךְ אֶת עַמּוֹ יִשְׂרָאֵל בַּשָּׁלוֹם.

A Closer Look

The last prayer in the *Shemoneh Esrei* is a prayer for peace. We ask for many other things in our prayers, but without peace, people cannot live a normal life. Our Sages teach us that peace is the greatest blessing.

When we are closer to Hashem, we become happier and more at peace with ourselves.

My God, keep me from talking bad about people and speaking dishonestly. If anyone curses me, let me ignore them and not care. Make me understand Your Torah, and make me want to do Your commandments. If anyone wants to do evil towards me, please stop him. Do this for Your sake and for the sake of Your Torah. So the ones You love should be at peace, please answer me! May my words and thoughts be favorable to You, Hashem.

אֱלֹהַי, נְצוֹר לְשׁוֹנִי מֵרָע, וּשְׂפָתַי מִדַּבֵּר מִרְמָה, וְלִמְקַלְלַי נַפְשִׁי תִדּוֹם, וְנַפְשִׁי כֶּעָפָר לַכֹּל תִּהְיֶה. פְּתַח לִבִּי בְּתוֹרָתֶךָ, וּבְמִצְוֹתֶיךָ תִּרְדּוֹף נַפְשִׁי. וְכָל הַחוֹשְׁבִים עָלַי רָעָה, מְהֵרָה הָפֵר עֲצָתָם וְקַלְקֵל מַחֲשַׁבְתָּם. עֲשֵׂה לְמַעַן שְׁמֶךָ, עֲשֵׂה לְמַעַן יְמִינֶךָ, עֲשֵׂה לְמַעַן קְדֻשָּׁתֶךָ, עֲשֵׂה לְמַעַן תּוֹרָתֶךָ. לְמַעַן יֵחָלְצוּן יְדִידֶיךָ, הוֹשִׁיעָה יְמִינְךָ וַעֲנֵנִי. יִהְיוּ לְרָצוֹן אִמְרֵי פִי וְהֶגְיוֹן לִבִּי לְפָנֶיךָ, יהוה צוּרִי וְגֹאֲלִי.

Take three steps while bowing, then bow to the left and say:

Hashem, Who makes peace in the heavens,

עֹשֶׂה שָׁלוֹם בִּמְרוֹמָיו,

Bow to the right and say:

may He make peace upon us,

הוּא יַעֲשֶׂה שָׁלוֹם עָלֵינוּ,

Bow forward and say:

and upon all of Israel. Let us say, Amen.

וְעַל כָּל יִשְׂרָאֵל. וְאִמְרוּ: אָמֵן.

Straighten up and say:

May it be Your will, Hashem, our God, and the God of our fathers, that the *Beis HaMikdash* be rebuilt quickly, in our lifetime. Let us have a share of Your Torah. And may we serve You with fear, as we did in the past. And may the offerings of the Jewish people and Jerusalem be desired by Hashem, as in the past.

יְהִי רָצוֹן מִלְּפָנֶיךָ, יהוה אֱלֹהֵינוּ וֵאלֹהֵי אֲבוֹתֵינוּ, שֶׁיִּבָּנֶה בֵּית הַמִּקְדָּשׁ בִּמְהֵרָה בְיָמֵינוּ, וְתֵן חֶלְקֵנוּ בְּתוֹרָתֶךָ. וְשָׁם נַעֲבָדְךָ בְּיִרְאָה, כִּימֵי עוֹלָם וּכְשָׁנִים קַדְמוֹנִיּוֹת. וְעָרְבָה לַיהוה מִנְחַת יְהוּדָה וִירוּשָׁלָיִם, כִּימֵי עוֹלָם וּכְשָׁנִים קַדְמוֹנִיּוֹת.

A Closer Look
We finish the *Shemoneh Esrei* with a short prayer, hoping that Hashem accepts our prayers.
When we pray we open up our heart. When we have an open heart, Hashem can help us with our problems.

עָלֵינוּ / *Aleinu*

We stand while reciting this prayer:

We should praise Hashem, the Master of everything, and speak greatness of He Who created everything. For He did not make us like the other nations. They bow down and pray to nothing.

עָלֵינוּ לְשַׁבֵּחַ לַאֲדוֹן הַכֹּל, לָתֵת גְּדֻלָּה לְיוֹצֵר בְּרֵאשִׁית, שֶׁלֹּא עָשָׂנוּ כְּגוֹיֵי הָאֲרָצוֹת, וְלֹא שָׂמָנוּ כְּמִשְׁפְּחוֹת הָאֲדָמָה. שֶׁלֹּא שָׂם חֶלְקֵנוּ כָּהֶם, וְגוֹרָלֵנוּ כְּכָל הֲמוֹנָם. (שֶׁהֵם מִשְׁתַּחֲוִים לְהֶבֶל וָרִיק, וּמִתְפַּלְלִים אֶל אֵל לֹא יוֹשִׁיעַ.)

But we bow and give thanks to the King of all kings, the Holy One, Blessed is He. Hashem spreads out the heavens and establishes the earth. Hashem is in Heaven. He is our God, there is no other. Our King is true, there is no other besides Him.

As it is written in His Torah: You will know this day, and realize it in your heart, that Hashem is the only God in the Heavens above and on the earth below. There is no other god.

Therefore, we place our hope in You, Hashem, our God, that we may soon see Your full glory, and be rid of the horrible idolatry that is on the earth. The world will be perfect under Hashem's rule. All the people of the world will call out Your Name, and the wicked people will turn towards You. All the people of the world will know that they should bow and swear only to You. Only before You will they bow, and to Your Name they will give honor. And they will all accept You as their King, forever. For the kingdom is Yours and You will rule forever.

And it is written in the Torah: Hashem will be King forever. And it is said (in the Prophets): And on that day Hashem will be One and His Name will be One.

וַאֲנַחְנוּ כּוֹרְעִים וּמִשְׁתַּחֲוִים וּמוֹדִים, לִפְנֵי מֶלֶךְ מַלְכֵי הַמְּלָכִים הַקָּדוֹשׁ בָּרוּךְ הוּא. שֶׁהוּא נוֹטֶה שָׁמַיִם וְיֹסֵד אָרֶץ, וּמוֹשַׁב יְקָרוֹ בַּשָּׁמַיִם מִמַּעַל, וּשְׁכִינַת עֻזּוֹ בְּגָבְהֵי מְרוֹמִים. הוּא אֱלֹהֵינוּ, אֵין עוֹד. אֱמֶת מַלְכֵּנוּ, אֶפֶס זוּלָתוֹ, כַּכָּתוּב בְּתוֹרָתוֹ: וְיָדַעְתָּ הַיּוֹם וַהֲשֵׁבֹתָ אֶל לְבָבֶךָ, כִּי יְהוָה הוּא הָאֱלֹהִים בַּשָּׁמַיִם מִמַּעַל וְעַל הָאָרֶץ מִתָּחַת, אֵין עוֹד.

עַל כֵּן נְקַוֶּה לְּךָ, יְהוָה אֱלֹהֵינוּ, לִרְאוֹת מְהֵרָה בְּתִפְאֶרֶת עֻזֶּךָ, לְהַעֲבִיר גִּלּוּלִים מִן הָאָרֶץ, וְהָאֱלִילִים כָּרוֹת יִכָּרֵתוּן, לְתַקֵּן עוֹלָם בְּמַלְכוּת שַׁדַּי. וְכָל בְּנֵי בָשָׂר יִקְרְאוּ בִשְׁמֶךָ, לְהַפְנוֹת אֵלֶיךָ כָּל רִשְׁעֵי אָרֶץ. יַכִּירוּ וְיֵדְעוּ כָּל יוֹשְׁבֵי תֵבֵל, כִּי לְךָ תִּכְרַע כָּל בֶּרֶךְ, תִּשָּׁבַע כָּל לָשׁוֹן. לְפָנֶיךָ יְהוָה אֱלֹהֵינוּ יִכְרְעוּ וְיִפֹּלוּ, וְלִכְבוֹד שִׁמְךָ יְקָר יִתֵּנוּ. וִיקַבְּלוּ כֻלָּם אֶת עוֹל מַלְכוּתֶךָ, וְתִמְלֹךְ עֲלֵיהֶם מְהֵרָה לְעוֹלָם וָעֶד. כִּי הַמַּלְכוּת שֶׁלְּךָ הִיא וּלְעוֹלְמֵי עַד תִּמְלוֹךְ בְּכָבוֹד, כַּכָּתוּב בְּתוֹרָתֶךָ: יְהוָה יִמְלֹךְ לְעֹלָם וָעֶד. וְנֶאֱמַר: וְהָיָה יְהוָה לְמֶלֶךְ עַל כָּל הָאָרֶץ, בַּיּוֹם הַהוּא יִהְיֶה יְהוָה אֶחָד וּשְׁמוֹ אֶחָד.

Did You Know??
    Aleinu is a very special prayer. The Midrash tells us that it was written by Yehoshua after he led the Jews across the Jordan River into Eretz Yisrael and destroyed the city of Yericho (Jericho).
    Our Sages tell us that when someone says *Aleinu*, the angels listen closely and say to Hashem, "What a special people You have!"

A Closer Look
    The first section of *Aleinu* explains how different our belief is from that of the rest of the world.
    The second section tells of our hope that all people will one day believe only in Hashem, the true God.

אֲנִי מַאֲמִין / Ani Ma'amin

1. I believe with complete faith that Hashem created everything and is in charge of all that He created. Only He made, makes, and will make everything exist.

א אֲנִי מַאֲמִין בֶּאֱמוּנָה שְׁלֵמָה, שֶׁהַבּוֹרֵא יִתְבָּרַךְ שְׁמוֹ הוּא בּוֹרֵא וּמַנְהִיג לְכָל הַבְּרוּאִים, וְהוּא לְבַדּוֹ עָשָׂה וְעוֹשֶׂה וְיַעֲשֶׂה לְכָל הַמַּעֲשִׂים.

2. I believe with complete faith that Hashem is the only One and there is nothing else like Him in any way. He alone is our God Who was, Who is, and Who will always be.

ב אֲנִי מַאֲמִין בֶּאֱמוּנָה שְׁלֵמָה, שֶׁהַבּוֹרֵא יִתְבָּרַךְ שְׁמוֹ הוּא יָחִיד וְאֵין יְחִידוּת כָּמוֹהוּ בְּשׁוּם פָּנִים, וְהוּא לְבַדּוֹ אֱלֹהֵינוּ, הָיָה הֹוֶה וְיִהְיֶה.

3. I believe with complete faith that Hashem has no body. He is not affected by physical things and has no form at all.

ג אֲנִי מַאֲמִין בֶּאֱמוּנָה שְׁלֵמָה, שֶׁהַבּוֹרֵא יִתְבָּרַךְ שְׁמוֹ אֵינוֹ גוּף, וְלֹא יַשִּׂיגוּהוּ מַשִּׂיגֵי הַגּוּף, וְאֵין לוֹ שׁוּם דִּמְיוֹן כְּלָל.

4. I believe with complete faith that Hashem is first and last; there was nothing before Him and there will be nothing after Him.

ד אֲנִי מַאֲמִין בֶּאֱמוּנָה שְׁלֵמָה, שֶׁהַבּוֹרֵא יִתְבָּרַךְ שְׁמוֹ הוּא רִאשׁוֹן וְהוּא אַחֲרוֹן.

5. I believe with complete faith that Hashem is the only One to whom we should pray. It is wrong to pray to anything else.

6. I believe with complete faith that all the words the prophets said are true.

7. I believe with complete faith that the prophecy of Moshe, our teacher, was true. He was the greatest of all prophets, including both the prophets who lived before him and the prophets who lived after him.

8. I believe with complete faith that the whole Torah that we now have is exactly the same as the one that was given to Moshe, our teacher (at Har Sinai).

9. I believe with complete faith that this Torah will not be changed, and there will never be another Torah from Hashem.

10. I believe with complete faith that Hashem knows everything that people do and everything that people think.

11. I believe with complete faith that Hashem rewards those who follow His mitzvos, and punishes those who sin.

12. I believe with complete faith in the coming of the Mashiach. Even if it will take a long time for him to come, I wait for him to come every day.

13. I believe with complete faith that the dead will be brought back to life when Hashem wants it to happen.

ה אֲנִי מַאֲמִין בֶּאֱמוּנָה שְׁלֵמָה, שֶׁהַבּוֹרֵא יִתְבָּרַךְ שְׁמוֹ לוֹ לְבַדּוֹ רָאוּי לְהִתְפַּלֵּל, וְאֵין לְזוּלָתוֹ רָאוּי לְהִתְפַּלֵּל.

ו אֲנִי מַאֲמִין בֶּאֱמוּנָה שְׁלֵמָה, שֶׁכָּל דִּבְרֵי נְבִיאִים אֱמֶת.

ז אֲנִי מַאֲמִין בֶּאֱמוּנָה שְׁלֵמָה, שֶׁנְּבוּאַת מֹשֶׁה רַבֵּנוּ עָלָיו הַשָּׁלוֹם הָיְתָה אֲמִתִּית, וְשֶׁהוּא הָיָה אָב לַנְּבִיאִים, לַקּוֹדְמִים לְפָנָיו וְלַבָּאִים אַחֲרָיו.

ח אֲנִי מַאֲמִין בֶּאֱמוּנָה שְׁלֵמָה, שֶׁכָּל הַתּוֹרָה הַמְּצוּיָה עַתָּה בְּיָדֵינוּ הִיא הַנְּתוּנָה לְמֹשֶׁה רַבֵּנוּ עָלָיו הַשָּׁלוֹם.

ט אֲנִי מַאֲמִין בֶּאֱמוּנָה שְׁלֵמָה, שֶׁזֹּאת הַתּוֹרָה לֹא תְהֵא מֻחְלֶפֶת וְלֹא תְהֵא תּוֹרָה אַחֶרֶת מֵאֵת הַבּוֹרֵא יִתְבָּרַךְ שְׁמוֹ.

י אֲנִי מַאֲמִין בֶּאֱמוּנָה שְׁלֵמָה, שֶׁהַבּוֹרֵא יִתְבָּרַךְ שְׁמוֹ יוֹדֵעַ כָּל מַעֲשֵׂה בְּנֵי אָדָם וְכָל מַחְשְׁבוֹתָם, שֶׁנֶּאֱמַר: הַיֹּצֵר יַחַד לִבָּם, הַמֵּבִין אֶל כָּל מַעֲשֵׂיהֶם.

יא אֲנִי מַאֲמִין בֶּאֱמוּנָה שְׁלֵמָה, שֶׁהַבּוֹרֵא יִתְבָּרַךְ שְׁמוֹ גּוֹמֵל טוֹב לְשׁוֹמְרֵי מִצְוֹתָיו וּמַעֲנִישׁ לְעוֹבְרֵי מִצְוֹתָיו.

יב אֲנִי מַאֲמִין בֶּאֱמוּנָה שְׁלֵמָה, בְּבִיאַת הַמָּשִׁיחַ וְאַף עַל פִּי שֶׁיִּתְמַהְמֵהַּ, עִם כָּל זֶה אֲחַכֶּה לּוֹ בְּכָל יוֹם שֶׁיָּבוֹא.

יג אֲנִי מַאֲמִין בֶּאֱמוּנָה שְׁלֵמָה, שֶׁתִּהְיֶה תְּחִיַּת הַמֵּתִים בְּעֵת שֶׁיַּעֲלֶה רָצוֹן מֵאֵת הַבּוֹרֵא יִתְבָּרַךְ שְׁמוֹ וְיִתְעַלֶּה זִכְרוֹ לָעַד וּלְנֵצַח נְצָחִים.

Did You Know??
The Rambam listed these "Thirteen Principles of Faith." The Rambam said that everyone should study them each day because they are the basic and most important points of our belief in Hashem.
The Rambam also teaches that we must pray every day. It is fifth of the 613 mitzvos.

A Closer Look
For us to do mitzvos properly, we must first believe in Hashem and that He is the One Who is commanding us to do the mitzvos.

The prayer יִגְדַּל that we say every day is very similar to the Thirteen Principles of Faith that we say in אֲנִי מַאֲמִין.

בִּרְכַּת הַמָּזוֹן / *Grace After Meals*

On Shabbos and holidays, we recite the following psalm before *Bircas HaMazon*:

A song that the *Leviim* used to sing on the steps of the *Beis HaMikdash:* When Hashem will bring back the exiles to Eretz Yisrael, it will be like a dream come true. We will be filled with laughter and song. The other nations will declare, ''Hashem has done great things for His people.'' Hashem has done great things for us — we will be happy. Hashem, please bring our people back to Eretz Yisrael, so it will be like a dry land that becomes filled with flowing springs. Let our people be like the farmers who plant seeds with tears, but are filled with joy when they harvest the crops. Let our people be like the one who cries when he carries his seeds to the field, but is joyous when he comes back carrying his bundles.

I will praise Hashem and may everyone bless Hashem forever. Let us give thanks to Hashem for He is good. He is always kind. Who can retell the miracles He does? Who can say all His praise?

שִׁיר הַמַּעֲלוֹת, בְּשׁוּב יהוה אֶת שִׁיבַת צִיּוֹן, הָיִינוּ כְּחֹלְמִים. אָז יִמָּלֵא שְׂחוֹק פִּינוּ וּלְשׁוֹנֵנוּ רִנָּה, אָז יֹאמְרוּ בַגּוֹיִם, הִגְדִּיל יהוה לַעֲשׂוֹת עִם אֵלֶּה. הִגְדִּיל יהוה לַעֲשׂוֹת עִמָּנוּ, הָיִינוּ שְׂמֵחִים. שׁוּבָה יהוה אֶת שְׁבִיתֵנוּ כַּאֲפִיקִים בַּנֶּגֶב. הַזֹּרְעִים בְּדִמְעָה בְּרִנָּה יִקְצֹרוּ. הָלוֹךְ יֵלֵךְ וּבָכֹה נֹשֵׂא מֶשֶׁךְ הַזָּרַע, בֹּא יָבֹא בְרִנָּה נֹשֵׂא אֲלֻמֹּתָיו.

תְּהִלַּת יהוה יְדַבֶּר פִּי, וִיבָרֵךְ כָּל בָּשָׂר שֵׁם קָדְשׁוֹ לְעוֹלָם וָעֶד. וַאֲנַחְנוּ נְבָרֵךְ יָהּ, מֵעַתָּה וְעַד עוֹלָם, הַלְלוּיָהּ. הוֹדוּ לַיהוה כִּי טוֹב, כִּי לְעוֹלָם חַסְדּוֹ. מִי יְמַלֵּל גְּבוּרוֹת יהוה, יַשְׁמִיעַ כָּל תְּהִלָּתוֹ.

If there are three or more males aged thirteen or older who have eaten together, one of them formally invites everyone to join in saying *Bircas HaMazon*. The leader of *Bircas HaMazon* begins his invitation:

רַבּוֹתַי נְבָרֵךְ.

Gentlemen, let us bless.

Everyone else answers:

יְהִי שֵׁם יהוה מְבֹרָךְ מֵעַתָּה וְעַד עוֹלָם.

May Hashem's Name be blessed, from now to forever.

The leader continues (if ten men join, the words in parentheses are included):

יְהִי שֵׁם יהוה מְבֹרָךְ מֵעַתָּה וְעַד עוֹלָם.

May Hashem's Name be blessed, from now to forever.

בִּרְשׁוּת מָרָנָן וְרַבָּנָן וְרַבּוֹתַי, נְבָרֵךְ (אֱלֹהֵינוּ) שֶׁאָכַלְנוּ מִשֶּׁלּוֹ.

With the permission of the honored people here, let us bless (our God) Whose food we have eaten.

Everyone else answers:

בָּרוּךְ (אֱלֹהֵינוּ) שֶׁאָכַלְנוּ מִשֶּׁלּוֹ וּבְטוּבוֹ חָיִינוּ.

Blessed is He (our God) from Whose food we have eaten and through Whose goodness we live.

The leader continues:

בָּרוּךְ (אֱלֹהֵינוּ) שֶׁאָכַלְנוּ מִשֶּׁלּוֹ וּבְטוּבוֹ חָיִינוּ.

Blessed is He (our God) from Whose food we have eaten and through Whose goodness we live.

All continue:

בָּרוּךְ הוּא וּבָרוּךְ שְׁמוֹ.

Blessed is He and blessed is His Name.

52

FIRST BLESSING

Blessed are You, Hashem, our God, King of the universe, Who feeds the entire world with His goodness, with love, with kindness and with mercy. He gives food to everyone because His kindness is forever. Since He is so good, we have always had enough food. May He make sure that we always have enough food. We ask for this so that we can praise His great Name, because He is the God Who feeds everyone and does good for everyone. He prepares food for everything He has created. Blessed are You, Hashem, Who feeds everyone.

בָּרוּךְ אַתָּה יהוה אֱלֹהֵינוּ מֶלֶךְ הָעוֹלָם, הַזָּן אֶת הָעוֹלָם כֻּלוֹ, בְּטוּבוֹ, בְּחֵן בְּחֶסֶד וּבְרַחֲמִים, הוּא נֹתֵן לֶחֶם לְכָל בָּשָׂר, כִּי לְעוֹלָם חַסְדּוֹ. וּבְטוּבוֹ הַגָּדוֹל, תָּמִיד לֹא חָסַר לָנוּ, וְאַל יֶחְסַר לָנוּ מָזוֹן לְעוֹלָם וָעֶד. בַּעֲבוּר שְׁמוֹ הַגָּדוֹל, כִּי הוּא אֵל זָן וּמְפַרְנֵס לַכֹּל, וּמֵטִיב לַכֹּל, וּמֵכִין מָזוֹן לְכָל בְּרִיּוֹתָיו אֲשֶׁר בָּרָא. בָּרוּךְ אַתָּה יהוה, הַזָּן אֶת הַכֹּל.

Did You Know??

Moshe wrote this blessing to thank God for giving the Jews the manna (מָן) to eat in the desert after they left Egypt.

We are commanded by the Torah to say *Bircas HaMazon*. It says in the Torah, "You shall eat, you shall be satisfied, and you shall bless Hashem, your God."

It is customary to leave some bread from the meal on the table when we say *Bircas HaMazon*. This is to remind us to thank Hashem for giving us so much food that there is even some left over.

A Closer Look

This is the first of four blessings in *Bircas HaMazon*. We thank Hashem for feeding us and the whole world.

This first blessing is called "*Bircas HaZan,* the Blessing for the Food."

SECOND BLESSING

נוֹדֶה לְךָ, יהוה אֱלֹהֵינוּ, עַל שֶׁהִנְחַלְתָּ לַאֲבוֹתֵינוּ אֶרֶץ חֶמְדָּה טוֹבָה וּרְחָבָה. וְעַל שֶׁהוֹצֵאתָנוּ יהוה אֱלֹהֵינוּ מֵאֶרֶץ מִצְרַיִם, וּפְדִיתָנוּ מִבֵּית עֲבָדִים, וְעַל בְּרִיתְךָ שֶׁחָתַמְתָּ בִּבְשָׂרֵנוּ, וְעַל תּוֹרָתְךָ שֶׁלִּמַּדְתָּנוּ, וְעַל חֻקֶּיךָ שֶׁהוֹדַעְתָּנוּ, וְעַל חַיִּים חֵן וָחֶסֶד שֶׁחוֹנַנְתָּנוּ, וְעַל אֲכִילַת מָזוֹן שָׁאַתָּה זָן וּמְפַרְנֵס אוֹתָנוּ תָּמִיד, בְּכָל יוֹם וּבְכָל עֵת וּבְכָל שָׁעָה.

We thank You, Hashem, our God, for giving Eretz Yisrael, a beautiful and good land, to our ancestors to be ours.

We thank You for taking us out of Egypt where we were slaves; for the mitzvah of *bris milah;* for teaching us Your Torah; for the mitzvos that You told us; and for the life, love and kindness that You have given us; and for the food You prepare for us every day, always.

On Chanukah and Purim we add *Al HaNissim.*
Turn to page 44.

וְעַל הַכֹּל, יהוה אֱלֹהֵינוּ, אֲנַחְנוּ מוֹדִים לָךְ, וּמְבָרְכִים אוֹתָךְ, יִתְבָּרַךְ שִׁמְךָ בְּפִי כָּל חַי תָּמִיד לְעוֹלָם וָעֶד. כַּכָּתוּב, וְאָכַלְתָּ וְשָׂבָעְתָּ, וּבֵרַכְתָּ אֶת יהוה אֱלֹהֶיךָ, עַל הָאָרֶץ הַטֹּבָה אֲשֶׁר נָתַן לָךְ. בָּרוּךְ אַתָּה יהוה, עַל הָאָרֶץ וְעַל הַמָּזוֹן.

For everything, Hashem, our God, we thank You and bless You.

May Your Name always be blessed by everyone, as it is written in the Torah, "You will eat, you will be satisfied, and then you will bless Hashem, your God, for the good land that He gave you." Blessed are You, Hashem, for the land and for the food.

Did You Know??
Yehoshua wrote this blessing when he led the Jews into Eretz Yisrael. Till now, the Jews had been eating manna in the desert, and now, for the first time in forty years, the Jews began to eat food from the land.

A Closer Look
This is the second blessing. We thank Hashem for giving us Eretz Yisrael and the mitzvos of the Torah.
The second blessing is called "*Bircas HaAretz,* the Blessing of the Land of Israel."

THIRD BLESSING

Hashem, our God, please have mercy on Your nation Israel; on Jerusalem, Your city; on the Temple Mount, the place of Your Glory; on the kingdom of David, Your king; and on the holy *Beis HaMikdash* which is called by Your Name. Our God, our Father, take care of us, feed us, support us, give us what we need, and make our lives easier. Hashem, our God, give us relief now from our troubles. Please, Hashem, our God, don't make us need gifts or even loans from other people; let us get all our needs from Your hand, which is open, holy, and generous. Then we will never feel ashamed or embarrassed.

רַחֵם יהוה אֱלֹהֵינוּ עַל יִשְׂרָאֵל עַמֶּךָ, וְעַל יְרוּשָׁלַיִם עִירֶךָ, וְעַל צִיּוֹן מִשְׁכַּן כְּבוֹדֶךָ, וְעַל מַלְכוּת בֵּית דָּוִד מְשִׁיחֶךָ, וְעַל הַבַּיִת הַגָּדוֹל וְהַקָּדוֹשׁ שֶׁנִּקְרָא שִׁמְךָ עָלָיו. אֱלֹהֵינוּ אָבִינוּ, רְעֵנוּ זוּנֵנוּ פַּרְנְסֵנוּ וְכַלְכְּלֵנוּ וְהַרְוִיחֵנוּ, וְהַרְוַח לָנוּ יהוה אֱלֹהֵינוּ מְהֵרָה מִכָּל צָרוֹתֵינוּ. וְנָא אַל תַּצְרִיכֵנוּ, יהוה אֱלֹהֵינוּ, לֹא לִידֵי מַתְּנַת בָּשָׂר וָדָם, וְלֹא לִידֵי הַלְוָאָתָם, כִּי אִם לְיָדְךָ הַמְּלֵאָה הַפְּתוּחָה הַקְּדוֹשָׁה וְהָרְחָבָה, שֶׁלֹּא נֵבוֹשׁ וְלֹא נִכָּלֵם לְעוֹלָם וָעֶד.

Did You Know??
The third blessing is called "Bircas Binyan Yerushalayim, the Blessing of the Building of Jerusalem."

A Closer Look
This is the beginning of the third blessing. We ask Hashem to have mercy on us and to rebuild Jerusalem and the *Beis HaMikdash*.

On Shabbos we recite this paragraph:

Please, Hashem, our God, make us strong through Your mitzvos and through this special mitzvah of the great and holy Shabbos. This is a great and holy day for us to rest on, as You have commanded. Please, Hashem, our God, calm us, and let there not be any trouble or sadness on this day of rest. Hashem, let us see Your city Zion comforted. Let us see Your holy city Jerusalem being rebuilt, because only You have the power to help and to comfort.

רְצֵה וְהַחֲלִיצֵנוּ יהוה אֱלֹהֵינוּ בְּמִצְוֹתֶיךָ, וּבְמִצְוַת יוֹם הַשְּׁבִיעִי הַשַּׁבָּת הַגָּדוֹל וְהַקָּדוֹשׁ הַזֶּה, כִּי יוֹם זֶה גָּדוֹל וְקָדוֹשׁ הוּא לְפָנֶיךָ, לִשְׁבָּת בּוֹ וְלָנוּחַ בּוֹ בְּאַהֲבָה כְּמִצְוַת רְצוֹנֶךָ. וּבִרְצוֹנְךָ הָנִיחַ לָנוּ, יהוה אֱלֹהֵינוּ, שֶׁלֹּא תְהֵא צָרָה וְיָגוֹן וַאֲנָחָה בְּיוֹם מְנוּחָתֵנוּ. וְהַרְאֵנוּ יהוה אֱלֹהֵינוּ בְּנֶחָמַת צִיּוֹן עִירֶךָ, וּבְבִנְיַן יְרוּשָׁלַיִם עִיר קָדְשֶׁךָ, כִּי אַתָּה הוּא בַּעַל הַיְשׁוּעוֹת וּבַעַל הַנֶּחָמוֹת.

55

אֱלֹהֵינוּ וֵאלֹהֵי אֲבוֹתֵינוּ, יַעֲלֶה, וְיָבֹא, וְיַגִּיעַ, וְיֵרָאֶה, וְיֵרָצֶה, וְיִשָּׁמַע, וְיִפָּקֵד, וְיִזָּכֵר, זִכְרוֹנֵנוּ וּפִקְדוֹנֵנוּ, וְזִכְרוֹן אֲבוֹתֵינוּ, וְזִכְרוֹן מָשִׁיחַ בֶּן דָּוִד עַבְדֶּךָ, וְזִכְרוֹן יְרוּשָׁלַיִם עִיר קָדְשֶׁךָ, וְזִכְרוֹן כָּל עַמְּךָ בֵּית יִשְׂרָאֵל לְפָנֶיךָ, לִפְלֵיטָה לְטוֹבָה לְחֵן וּלְחֶסֶד וּלְרַחֲמִים, לְחַיִּים וּלְשָׁלוֹם, בְּיוֹם

Our God and God of our fathers, we pray that the following thoughts will be heard and recalled by You: memories of us; of our fathers; of Mashiach, from the family of David; of Jerusalem, Your holy city; and of the entire nation of Israel. Remember all these to rescue us, to give us goodness, love, and kindness, life and peace, on this day of

on Rosh Chodesh say:

Rosh Chodesh, רֹאשׁ הַחֹדֶשׁ הַזֶּה.

on Pesach say:

the Festival of Matzos, חַג הַמַּצּוֹת הַזֶּה.

on Shavuos say:

the Shavuos Festival חַג הַשָּׁבֻעוֹת הַזֶּה.

on Rosh Hashanah say:

Remembrance הַזִּכָּרוֹן הַזֶּה.

on Succos say:

the Succos Festival חַג הַסֻּכּוֹת הַזֶּה.

on Shemini Atzeres and Simchas Torah say:

the Shemini Atzeres Festival הַשְּׁמִינִי חַג הָעֲצֶרֶת הַזֶּה.

Remember us, Hashem, our God, for good, for blessing, and for life. Have pity on us and save us, because we look to You for help since You are the generous God, filled with mercy.

זָכְרֵנוּ יהוה אֱלֹהֵינוּ בּוֹ לְטוֹבָה, וּפָקְדֵנוּ בוֹ לִבְרָכָה, וְהוֹשִׁיעֵנוּ בוֹ לְחַיִּים. וּבִדְבַר יְשׁוּעָה וְרַחֲמִים, חוּס וְחָנֵּנוּ וְרַחֵם עָלֵינוּ וְהוֹשִׁיעֵנוּ, כִּי אֵלֶיךָ עֵינֵינוּ, כִּי אֵל (מֶלֶךְ) חַנּוּן וְרַחוּם אָתָּה.

A Closer Look
In יַעֲלֶה וְיָבֹא we ask Hashem to remember us for good things, as He did in the days of old when we brought special offerings on Rosh Chodesh and the holidays.

And please rebuild Jerusalem, the holy city, quickly, in our lifetime. Blessed are You, Hashem, Who builds Jerusalem with mercy. Amen.

וּבְנֵה יְרוּשָׁלַיִם עִיר הַקֹּדֶשׁ בִּמְהֵרָה בְיָמֵינוּ. בָּרוּךְ אַתָּה יהוה, בּוֹנֵה (בְּרַחֲמָיו) יְרוּשָׁלָיִם. אָמֵן.

FOURTH BLESSING

Blessed are You, Hashem, our God, King of the universe, God Who is our Father, our King, our Master; Who created us, Who saved us, Who made us; our Holy One, the Holy One of Yaakov our forefather; our Shepherd, the Shepherd of Israel; the King Who is good and Who does good to everyone. Every single day He *did* good, He *does* good, and He *will do* good for us. He *gave* us much, He *gives* us much, and He *will give* us much forever; with love, kindness, and with much help, success, blessing, comfort, support, mercy, life and peace. May we never lack any good things.

בָּרוּךְ אַתָּה יהוה אֱלֹהֵינוּ מֶלֶךְ הָעוֹלָם, הָאֵל אָבִינוּ מַלְכֵּנוּ אַדִּירֵנוּ בּוֹרְאֵנוּ גּוֹאֲלֵנוּ יוֹצְרֵנוּ. קְדוֹשֵׁנוּ קְדוֹשׁ יַעֲקֹב, רוֹעֵנוּ רוֹעֵה יִשְׂרָאֵל, הַמֶּלֶךְ הַטּוֹב וְהַמֵּטִיב לַכֹּל, שֶׁבְּכָל יוֹם וָיוֹם הוּא הֵטִיב, הוּא מֵטִיב, הוּא יֵיטִיב לָנוּ. הוּא גְמָלָנוּ, הוּא גוֹמְלֵנוּ, הוּא יִגְמְלֵנוּ לָעַד, לְחֵן וּלְחֶסֶד וּלְרַחֲמִים וּלְרֶוַח הַצָּלָה וְהַצְלָחָה, בְּרָכָה וִישׁוּעָה נֶחָמָה פַּרְנָסָה וְכַלְכָּלָה וְרַחֲמִים וְחַיִּים וְשָׁלוֹם וְכָל טוֹב, וּמִכָּל טוּב לְעוֹלָם אַל יְחַסְּרֵנוּ.

Did You Know??
Rabban Gamliel wrote this blessing in the city of Yavneh after the second *Beis HaMikdash* was destroyed.

A Closer Look
This is the fourth blessing. We thank Hashem because He has always been good to us, is good to us, and will always be good to us.
The blessing is called "HaTov VeHaMeitiv," Who is good and does good.

May the Merciful God always be our King. May the Merciful God be blessed in heaven and on Earth. May the Merciful God be praised in every generation, and always be proud of us and honored by the way we act. May the Merciful God support us with honor. May the Merciful God stop all our suffering and lead us proudly to our land, Eretz Yisrael. May the Merciful God send much blessing into this house and on this table upon which we have eaten. May the Merciful God send us Eliyahu the Prophet, who is remembered for doing good, and may he bring us good news, to save us and comfort us.

הָרַחֲמָן הוּא יִמְלוֹךְ עָלֵינוּ לְעוֹלָם וָעֶד. הָרַחֲמָן הוּא יִתְבָּרַךְ בַּשָּׁמַיִם וּבָאָרֶץ. הָרַחֲמָן הוּא יִשְׁתַּבַּח לְדוֹר דּוֹרִים, וְיִתְפָּאַר בָּנוּ לָעַד וּלְנֵצַח נְצָחִים, וְיִתְהַדַּר בָּנוּ לָעַד וּלְעוֹלְמֵי עוֹלָמִים. הָרַחֲמָן הוּא יְפַרְנְסֵנוּ בְּכָבוֹד. הָרַחֲמָן הוּא יִשְׁבּוֹר עֻלֵּנוּ מֵעַל צַוָּארֵנוּ, וְהוּא יוֹלִיכֵנוּ קוֹמְמִיּוּת לְאַרְצֵנוּ. הָרַחֲמָן הוּא יִשְׁלַח לָנוּ בְּרָכָה מְרֻבָּה בַּבַּיִת הַזֶּה, וְעַל שֻׁלְחָן זֶה שֶׁאָכַלְנוּ עָלָיו. הָרַחֲמָן הוּא יִשְׁלַח לָנוּ אֶת אֵלִיָּהוּ הַנָּבִיא זָכוּר לַטּוֹב, וִיבַשֶּׂר לָנוּ בְּשׂוֹרוֹת טוֹבוֹת יְשׁוּעוֹת וְנֶחָמוֹת.

May it be God's will that this host not be embarrassed either in this world or in the World to Come. May he be successful in everything that he does and may it be easy for him to earn a living. May he never be led into sin or into wicked thought.

יְהִי רָצוֹן שֶׁלֹּא יֵבוֹשׁ וְלֹא יִכָּלֵם בַּעַל הַבַּיִת הַזֶּה, לֹא בָעוֹלָם הַזֶּה וְלֹא בָעוֹלָם הַבָּא, וְיַצְלִיחַ בְּכָל נְכָסָיו, וְיִהְיוּ נְכָסָיו מֻצְלָחִים וּקְרוֹבִים לָעִיר, וְאַל יִשְׁלוֹט שָׂטָן בְּמַעֲשֵׂה יָדָיו, וְאַל יִזְדַּקֵּק לְפָנָיו שׁוּם דְּבַר חֵטְא וְהִרְהוּר עָוֹן, מֵעַתָּה וְעַד עוֹלָם.

May the Merciful God bless my father and teacher, the head of this house, and my mother and teacher, the lady of this house; may He bless them, their home, their children and everything they have,

הָרַחֲמָן הוּא יְבָרֵךְ אֶת אָבִי מוֹרִי בַּעַל הַבַּיִת הַזֶּה, וְאֶת אִמִּי מוֹרָתִי בַּעֲלַת הַבַּיִת הַזֶּה, אוֹתָם וְאֶת בֵּיתָם וְאֶת זַרְעָם וְאֶת כָּל אֲשֶׁר לָהֶם.

May the Merciful God bless me (and my spouse and my children) and all that is mine,

הָרַחֲמָן הוּא יְבָרֵךְ אוֹתִי (וְאֶת אִשְׁתִּי / וְאֶת בַּעְלִי. וְאֶת זַרְעִי) וְאֶת כָּל אֲשֶׁר לִי.

May the Merciful God bless the head of this house and the lady of this house; may He bless them, their home, their children and everything they have,

הָרַחֲמָן הוּא יְבָרֵךְ אֶת בַּעַל הַבַּיִת הַזֶּה, וְאֶת בַּעֲלַת הַבַּיִת הַזֶּה, אוֹתָם וְאֶת בֵּיתָם וְאֶת זַרְעָם וְאֶת כָּל אֲשֶׁר לָהֶם.

us, and everything that we have, just as our forefathers Avraham, Yitzchak and Yaakov were blessed with everything, may He bless us also with everything. Amen.

אוֹתָנוּ וְאֶת כָּל אֲשֶׁר לָנוּ, כְּמוֹ שֶׁנִּתְבָּרְכוּ אֲבוֹתֵינוּ אַבְרָהָם יִצְחָק וְיַעֲקֹב בַּכֹּל מִכֹּל כֹּל, כֵּן יְבָרֵךְ אוֹתָנוּ כֻּלָּנוּ יַחַד בִּבְרָכָה שְׁלֵמָה וְנֹאמַר, אָמֵן.

In Heaven above, may we and everyone with us be judged as deserving of peace. May we get a blessing and kindness from Hashem, and may Hashem and other people look at us with favor and with understanding.

בַּמָּרוֹם יְלַמְּדוּ עֲלֵיהֶם וְעָלֵינוּ זְכוּת, שֶׁתְּהֵא לְמִשְׁמֶרֶת שָׁלוֹם. וְנִשָּׂא בְרָכָה מֵאֵת יהוה, וּצְדָקָה מֵאֱלֹהֵי יִשְׁעֵנוּ, וְנִמְצָא חֵן וְשֵׂכֶל טוֹב בְּעֵינֵי אֱלֹהִים וְאָדָם.

On Shabbos we add:

May the Merciful God let us inherit the World to Come, which is a day that is all Shabbos, a day of complete rest, forever.

הָרַחֲמָן הוּא יַנְחִילֵנוּ יוֹם שֶׁכֻּלוֹ שַׁבָּת וּמְנוּחָה לְחַיֵּי הָעוֹלָמִים.

On Rosh Chodesh we add:

May the Merciful God renew this month with goodness and blessing.

הָרַחֲמָן הוּא יְחַדֵּשׁ עָלֵינוּ אֶת הַחֹדֶשׁ הַזֶּה לְטוֹבָה וְלִבְרָכָה.

On Holidays we add:

May the Merciful God let us inherit a day which is completely good.

הָרַחֲמָן הוּא יַנְחִילֵנוּ יוֹם שֶׁכֻּלוֹ טוֹב.

On Rosh Hashanah we add:

May the Merciful God renew this year with goodness and blessing.

הָרַחֲמָן הוּא יְחַדֵּשׁ עָלֵינוּ אֶת הַשָּׁנָה הַזֹּאת לְטוֹבָה וְלִבְרָכָה.

On Succos we add:

May the Merciful God build for us King David's fallen *succah* (the *Beis Hamikdash*).

הָרַחֲמָן הוּא יָקִים לָנוּ אֶת סֻכַּת דָּוִיד הַנֹּפֶלֶת.

May the Merciful God let us live until the Mashiach comes, and let us earn the life of the World to Come.

הָרַחֲמָן הוּא יְזַכֵּנוּ לִימוֹת הַמָּשִׁיחַ וּלְחַיֵּי הָעוֹלָם הַבָּא.

On weekdays we say:
Hashem performs great salvations and shows
On Shabbos, Rosh Chodesh, and Holidays we say:
Hashem is a tower of help and performs great

מַגְדִּל — On weekdays we say
מִגְדּוֹל — On Shabbos, Rosh Chodesh, and Holidays we say

kindness towards King David and his descendants forever. Hashem, Who makes peace in His Heavens, should please make peace for us and for all of Israel. Amen.

יְשׁוּעוֹת מַלְכּוֹ וְעֹשֶׂה חֶסֶד לִמְשִׁיחוֹ לְדָוִד וּלְזַרְעוֹ עַד עוֹלָם. עֹשֶׂה שָׁלוֹם בִּמְרוֹמָיו, הוּא יַעֲשֶׂה שָׁלוֹם עָלֵינוּ וְעַל כָּל יִשְׂרָאֵל. וְאִמְרוּ, אָמֵן.

You, who are holy to Hashem, should fear Him, because those who fear Him do not miss anything. Even strong young lions may go hungry, but if you try to be close to Hashem you will not be missing things that are good for you. Thank Hashem for He is good, and His kindness lasts forever. Please God, open up Your Hand and give everyone all that they desire. Blessed is the person who trusts in Hashem — for Hashem will protect him. I was young and now I am old, and in all my years, I never saw a *tzaddik* who was all alone and whose children had to beg for food. Hashem will give strength to His nation, Hashem will bless His nation with peace.

יְראוּ אֶת יהוה קְדֹשָׁיו, כִּי אֵין מַחְסוֹר לִירֵאָיו. כְּפִירִים רָשׁוּ וְרָעֵבוּ, וְדֹרְשֵׁי יהוה לֹא יַחְסְרוּ כָל טוֹב. הוֹדוּ לַיהוה כִּי טוֹב, כִּי לְעוֹלָם חַסְדּוֹ. פּוֹתֵחַ אֶת יָדֶךָ, וּמַשְׂבִּיעַ לְכָל חַי רָצוֹן. בָּרוּךְ הַגֶּבֶר אֲשֶׁר יִבְטַח בַּיהוה, וְהָיָה יהוה מִבְטַחוֹ. נַעַר הָיִיתִי גַּם זָקַנְתִּי, וְלֹא רָאִיתִי צַדִּיק נֶעֱזָב, וְזַרְעוֹ מְבַקֶּשׁ לָחֶם. יהוה עֹז לְעַמּוֹ יִתֵּן, יהוה יְבָרֵךְ אֶת עַמּוֹ בַשָּׁלוֹם.

עַל הַמִּחְיָה / Al HaMichyah

We say the following blessing after eating a certain minimum amount of
1) grains (such as cake or cereal), 2) wine or grape juice, 3) grapes, 4) figs, 5) pomegranates, 6) olives, or 7) dates.

Blessed are You, Hashem, our God, King of the universe,

בָּרוּךְ אַתָּה יהוה אֱלֹהֵינוּ מֶלֶךְ הָעוֹלָם,

After grains (such as cake or cereal):

for the nourishment and basic food,

עַל הַמִּחְיָה וְעַל הַכַּלְכָּלָה,

After wine or grape juice:

for the grapevine and the fruit of the grapevine,

עַל הַגֶּפֶן וְעַל פְּרִי הַגֶּפֶן,

After fruits (such as figs, pomegranates, olives or dates):

for the tree and the fruit of the tree,

עַל הָעֵץ וְעַל פְּרִי הָעֵץ,

and for all the food grown in the field. And for the wonderful, good land that You gave to our fathers, to eat from its fruit, and be satisfied from its goodness. Our God, have pity on Israel, Your nation, and on Jerusalem, Your city, and on Your Altar, and on Your *Beis HaMikdash*. Rebuild Jerusalem, the holy city, quickly, in our lifetime. Bring us to Jerusalem, and make us happy by rebuilding it. And let us eat the fruit of Eretz Yisrael and be satisfied with its goodness, and let us bless You for its holiness and purity.

וְעַל תְּנוּבַת הַשָּׂדֶה, וְעַל אֶרֶץ חֶמְדָּה טוֹבָה וּרְחָבָה, שֶׁרָצִיתָ וְהִנְחַלְתָּ לַאֲבוֹתֵינוּ, לֶאֱכוֹל מִפִּרְיָהּ וְלִשְׂבּוֹעַ מִטּוּבָהּ. רַחֵם נָא יהוה אֱלֹהֵינוּ עַל יִשְׂרָאֵל עַמֶּךָ, וְעַל יְרוּשָׁלַיִם עִירֶךָ, וְעַל צִיּוֹן מִשְׁכַּן כְּבוֹדֶךָ, וְעַל מִזְבְּחֶךָ וְעַל הֵיכָלֶךָ. וּבְנֵה יְרוּשָׁלַיִם עִיר הַקֹּדֶשׁ בִּמְהֵרָה בְיָמֵינוּ, וְהַעֲלֵנוּ לְתוֹכָהּ, וְשַׂמְּחֵנוּ בְּבִנְיָנָהּ, וְנֹאכַל מִפִּרְיָהּ, וְנִשְׂבַּע מִטּוּבָהּ, וּנְבָרֶכְךָ עָלֶיהָ בִּקְדֻשָּׁה וּבְטָהֳרָה.

Please, let us rest on this day of Shabbos.

וּרְצֵה וְהַחֲלִיצֵנוּ בְּיוֹם הַשַּׁבָּת הַזֶּה.

On Rosh Chodesh we add:

And remember us on this day of Rosh Chodesh.

וְזָכְרֵנוּ לְטוֹבָה בְּיוֹם רֹאשׁ הַחֹדֶשׁ הַזֶּה.

On Pesach:

And make us happy on this Holiday of Matzos (Pesach).

וְשַׂמְּחֵנוּ בְּיוֹם חַג הַמַּצּוֹת הַזֶּה.

On Shavuos:

And make us happy on this Holiday of Shavuos.

וְשַׂמְּחֵנוּ בְּיוֹם חַג הַשָּׁבְעוֹת הַזֶּה.

On Succos:

And make us happy on this Holiday of Succos.

וְשַׂמְּחֵנוּ בְּיוֹם חַג הַסֻּכּוֹת הַזֶּה.

On Shemini Atzeres and Simchas Torah:

And make us happy on this Holiday of Shemini Atzeres.

וְשַׂמְּחֵנוּ בְּיוֹם הַשְּׁמִינִי חַג הָעֲצֶרֶת הַזֶּה.

On Rosh Hashanah:

And remember us on this day of remembrance.

וְזָכְרֵנוּ לְטוֹבָה בְּיוֹם הַזִּכָּרוֹן הַזֶּה.

Because You, Hashem, are good, and do good to others, and we thank You

כִּי אַתָּה יהוה טוֹב וּמֵטִיב לַכֹּל, וְנוֹדֶה לְּךָ

After grains (such as cake or cereal):

for the land and for the nourishment.

עַל הָאָרֶץ וְעַל הַמִּחְיָה.

After wine or grape juice:

for the land and the fruit of the grapevine.

עַל הָאָרֶץ וְעַל פְּרִי הַגָּפֶן.

After fruits (such as figs, pomegranates, olives or dates):

for the land and the fruits.

עַל הָאָרֶץ וְעַל הַפֵּרוֹת.

Blessed are You, Hashem,

בָּרוּךְ אַתָּה יהוה,

After grains (such as cake or cereal):

for the land and for the nourishment.

עַל הָאָרֶץ וְעַל הַמִּחְיָה.

After wine or grape juice:

for the land and the fruit of the grapevine.

עַל הָאָרֶץ וְעַל פְּרִי הַגָּפֶן.

After fruits (such as figs, pomegranates, olives or dates):

for the land and the fruits.

עַל הָאָרֶץ וְעַל הַפֵּרוֹת.

Did You Know??
We make this *berachah* after eating the *Shiv'as HaMinim*, the Seven Special Types of Food. These are foods for which the Torah praises Eretz Yisrael. They are: wheat, barley (oats, rye, and spelt), grapes, figs, pomegranates, olives, and dates.

A Closer Look
Just like in *Bircas HaMazon*, we thank Hashem not only for creating humans, but for keeping all living things alive.

בּוֹרֵא נְפָשׁוֹת / Borei Nefashos

After eating or drinking any food for which we do not say either *Bircas HaMazon* or *Al HaMichyah*, we say the following:

Blessed are You, Hashem, our God, King of the universe, Who creates many living things with various needs. You keep alive whatever You create and provide them with whatever they need. Blessed is He, the life of the worlds.

בָּרוּךְ אַתָּה יהוה אֱלֹהֵינוּ מֶלֶךְ הָעוֹלָם, בּוֹרֵא נְפָשׁוֹת רַבּוֹת וְחֶסְרוֹנָן, עַל כָּל מַה שֶּׁבָּרָא(תָ) לְהַחֲיוֹת בָּהֶם נֶפֶשׁ כָּל חָי. בָּרוּךְ חֵי הָעוֹלָמִים.

בְּרָכוֹת שׁוֹנוֹת / Various Berachos

When we wash our hands before we eat bread, we say:

Blessed are You, Hashem, our God, King of the universe, Who has made us holy with His mitzvos, and commanded us about washing our hands.

בָּרוּךְ אַתָּה יהוה אֱלֹהֵינוּ מֶלֶךְ הָעוֹלָם, אֲשֶׁר קִדְּשָׁנוּ בְּמִצְוֹתָיו, וְצִוָּנוּ עַל נְטִילַת יָדֵים.

Before eating bread we say:

Blessed are You, Hashem, our God, King of the universe, Who brings bread out from the ground.

בָּרוּךְ אַתָּה יהוה אֱלֹהֵינוּ מֶלֶךְ הָעוֹלָם, הַמּוֹצִיא לֶחֶם מִן הָאָרֶץ.

Before eating grains, such as wheat products, barley, rye, oats, or spelt,
(for example cake, cookies, pretzels, spaghetti, and noodles) we say:

Blessed are You, Hashem, our God, King of the universe, Who creates different types of nourishment.

בָּרוּךְ אַתָּה יהוה אֱלֹהֵינוּ מֶלֶךְ הָעוֹלָם, בּוֹרֵא מִינֵי מְזוֹנוֹת.

Before drinking wine or grape juice we say:

Blessed are You, Hashem, our God, King of the universe, Who creates the fruit of the grapevine.

בָּרוּךְ אַתָּה יהוה אֱלֹהֵינוּ מֶלֶךְ הָעוֹלָם, בּוֹרֵא פְּרִי הַגָּפֶן.

Did You Know??
There are three types of *berachos*:
a. *berachos* said over things we benefit from (such as eating and drinking);
b. *berachos* said over mitzvos (such as *tzitzis, lulav,* and shofar);
c. *berachos* that just thank and praise Hashem (such as *Shemoneh Esrei,* and the blessings over thunder and lightning).
What these *berachos* have in common is that they all show our gratitude to Hashem for everything He does for us.

A Closer Look
Some foods are considered more important than others. That is why some foods receive their own *berachah*. For example, bread, which is considered the most important food, receives its own *berachah*. Grains, such as wheat and flour, receive a special *berachah*, *Borei Minei Mezonos*, because they, too, are considered a basic source of life.

Before eating fruit that grows on trees that have fruit year after year (for example, apples, pears, oranges, and olives) we say:

Blessed are You, Hashem, our God, King of the universe, Who creates the fruit of the tree.

בָּרוּךְ אַתָּה יהוה אֱלֹהֵינוּ מֶלֶךְ הָעוֹלָם, בּוֹרֵא פְּרִי הָעֵץ.

Before eating other foods that grow from the ground (such as watermelon, bananas, tomatoes, lettuce, and cucumbers) we say:

Blessed are You, Hashem, our God, King of the universe, Who creates the fruit of the ground.

בָּרוּךְ אַתָּה יהוה אֱלֹהֵינוּ מֶלֶךְ הָעוֹלָם, בּוֹרֵא פְּרִי הָאֲדָמָה.

Before eating or drinking any other food (such as meat, fish, eggs, ice cream, soda, and candy) we say:

Blessed are You, Hashem, our God, King of the universe, through Whose word everything is created.

בָּרוּךְ אַתָּה יהוה אֱלֹהֵינוּ מֶלֶךְ הָעוֹלָם, שֶׁהַכֹּל נִהְיֶה בִּדְבָרוֹ.

When we smell nice fragrances from a blend of spices we say:

Blessed are You, Hashem, our God, King of the universe, Who creates all the different types of spices and smells.

בָּרוּךְ אַתָּה יהוה אֱלֹהֵינוּ מֶלֶךְ הָעוֹלָם, בּוֹרֵא מִינֵי בְשָׂמִים.

Did You Know??
Not only is *Shehakol* the *berachah* to be said for many foods, but when someone is unsure about which *berachah* to recite, and there is no one there to ask, he should say *Shehakol*.

A Closer Look
People asked R' Zusha from Anipoli why he was always so happy and his wife was always so sad. "My wife looks to me to provide her with all that she needs," he explained. "I am not very good at that. I, on the other hand, look to Hashem to provide me with all that I need. And there is no greater provider than Hashem!"

Hashem provides us with everything that we need. When we make a *berachah* we thank Him for that.

When we hang up a *mezuzah* on a doorpost we say:

בָּרוּךְ אַתָּה יהוה אֱלֹהֵינוּ מֶלֶךְ הָעוֹלָם, אֲשֶׁר קִדְּשָׁנוּ בְּמִצְוֹתָיו וְצִוָּנוּ לִקְבֹּעַ מְזוּזָה.

Blessed are You, Hashem, our God, King of the universe, Who has made us holy with His mitzvos, and commanded us to hang up a mezuzah.

When we see lightning or other natural wonders we say:

בָּרוּךְ אַתָּה יהוה אֱלֹהֵינוּ מֶלֶךְ הָעוֹלָם, עֹשֶׂה מַעֲשֵׂה בְרֵאשִׁית.

Blessed are You, Hashem, our God, King of the universe, Who makes the works of creation.

When we hear thunder we say:

בָּרוּךְ אַתָּה יהוה אֱלֹהֵינוּ מֶלֶךְ הָעוֹלָם, שֶׁכֹּחוֹ וּגְבוּרָתוֹ מָלֵא עוֹלָם.

Blessed are You, Hashem, our God, King of the universe, Whose strength and power fill the entire universe.

When we see a rainbow in the sky we say:

בָּרוּךְ אַתָּה יהוה אֱלֹהֵינוּ מֶלֶךְ הָעוֹלָם, זוֹכֵר הַבְּרִית, וְנֶאֱמָן בִּבְרִיתוֹ, וְקַיָּם בְּמַאֲמָרוֹ.

Blessed are You, Hashem, our God, King of the universe, Who remembers the agreement He made with Noach not to destroy the world again, and does what He says He will do.

When we see the ocean we say:

בָּרוּךְ אַתָּה יהוה אֱלֹהֵינוּ מֶלֶךְ הָעוֹלָם, שֶׁעָשָׂה אֶת הַיָּם הַגָּדוֹל.

Blessed are You, Hashem, our God, King of the universe, Who made the great sea.

When we see a fruit tree begin to bloom (we say this *berachah* only once each year):

בָּרוּךְ אַתָּה יהוה אֱלֹהֵינוּ מֶלֶךְ הָעוֹלָם, שֶׁלֹּא חִסַּר בְּעוֹלָמוֹ דָּבָר, וּבָרָא בוֹ בְּרִיּוֹת טוֹבוֹת וְאִילָנוֹת טוֹבִים, לֵהָנוֹת בָּהֶם בְּנֵי אָדָם.

Blessed are You, Hashem, our God, King of the universe, Who created a universe that has everything, Who created in that universe good creatures and good trees, which give pleasure to man.

When we see a great Torah scholar we say:

Blessed are You, Hashem, our God, King of the universe, Who has given some of His knowledge to those people who fear Him.

בָּרוּךְ אַתָּה יהוה אֱלֹהֵינוּ מֶלֶךְ הָעוֹלָם, שֶׁחָלַק מֵחָכְמָתוֹ לִירֵאָיו.

When we eat a new fruit for the first time in the new season, or put on a new item of clothing for the first time, or do a seasonal mitzvah we say:

Blessed are You, Hashem, our God, King of the universe, for keeping us alive, taking care of us, and bringing us to this time.

בָּרוּךְ אַתָּה יהוה אֱלֹהֵינוּ מֶלֶךְ הָעוֹלָם, שֶׁהֶחֱיָנוּ וְקִיְּמָנוּ וְהִגִּיעָנוּ לַזְּמַן הַזֶּה.

When we hear very good news which benefits us and others we say:

Blessed are You, Hashem, our God, King of the universe, Who is good and does good.

בָּרוּךְ אַתָּה יהוה אֱלֹהֵינוּ מֶלֶךְ הָעוֹלָם, הַטּוֹב וְהַמֵּטִיב.

When we hear very bad news we say:

Blessed are You, Hashem, our God, King of the universe, Who is the true Judge.

בָּרוּךְ אַתָּה יהוה אֱלֹהֵינוּ מֶלֶךְ הָעוֹלָם, דַּיַּן הָאֱמֶת.

Did You Know??
Over 2,000 years ago, the *Anshei Knesses HaGedolah* made up the *berachos* in the exact form that we still have today.

A Closer Look
Everything in the world is really owned by Hashem. By making a *berachah,* we are thanking Him for letting us take what is really His.

קְרִיאַת שְׁמַע / **Bedtime Shema**

Before we go to sleep at night, we recite the *Shema*.

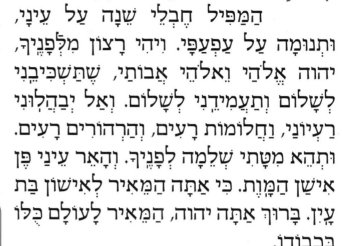

בָּרוּךְ אַתָּה יהוה אֱלֹהֵינוּ מֶלֶךְ הָעוֹלָם, הַמַּפִּיל חֶבְלֵי שֵׁנָה עַל עֵינַי, וּתְנוּמָה עַל עַפְעַפָּי. וִיהִי רָצוֹן מִלְּפָנֶיךָ, יהוה אֱלֹהַי וֵאלֹהֵי אֲבוֹתַי, שֶׁתַּשְׁכִּיבֵנִי לְשָׁלוֹם וְתַעֲמִידֵנִי לְשָׁלוֹם. וְאַל יְבַהֲלוּנִי רַעְיוֹנַי, וַחֲלוֹמוֹת רָעִים, וְהִרְהוּרִים רָעִים. וּתְהֵא מִטָּתִי שְׁלֵמָה לְפָנֶיךָ. וְהָאֵר עֵינַי פֶּן אִישַׁן הַמָּוֶת. כִּי אַתָּה הַמֵּאִיר לְאִישׁוֹן בַּת עָיִן. בָּרוּךְ אַתָּה יהוה, הַמֵּאִיר לָעוֹלָם כֻּלּוֹ בִּכְבוֹדוֹ.

Blessed are You, Hashem, our God, King of the universe, Who puts me to sleep.

Please, Hashem, put me to sleep peacefully and let me wake up peacefully. Please, do not let bad dreams and bad thoughts bother me while I sleep. Light up my eyes in the morning, Hashem, so I should wake up, because it is You Who allow people to wake up and see the world. Blessed are You, Hashem, Who lights up the whole world with His glory.

Did You Know??
We are not allowed to eat, drink, or talk after we say *HaMapil*. We should go right to sleep.

A Closer Look
Before we go to sleep at night, we should first examine what kind of day we had. Did we do nice things for other people? Did we do mitzvos? Is there anything we did wrong? We should ask Hashem to forgive us for anything we did wrong, and we should forgive others for anything not nice that they did to us.

We cover our eyes with our right hand. Then we say:

אֵל מֶלֶךְ נֶאֱמָן.

God, trustworthy King.

שְׁמַע יִשְׂרָאֵל, יהוה אֱלֹהֵינוּ, יהוה אֶחָד:

Hear, O Israel, Hashem is our God, Hashem is the only One.

We then say these words quietly:

בָּרוּךְ שֵׁם כְּבוֹד מַלְכוּתוֹ לְעוֹלָם וָעֶד.

Blessed is the Name of His wonderful kingdom forever and ever.

You shall love Hashem, your God, with your whole heart, with your whole soul, and with everything you own.

These things that I command you to-day shall always be in your heart.

You shall teach them to your children.

You should speak about them while you are sitting in your home, while you are walking in the street, when you go to sleep, and when you wake up.

Tie them as a sign upon your arm and let them be between your eyes.

Write them on the doorposts of your house and on your gates.

וְאָהַבְתָּ אֵת יהוה ׀ אֱלֹהֶיךָ, בְּכָל-לְבָבְךָ, וּבְכָל-נַפְשְׁךָ, וּבְכָל-מְאֹדֶךָ: וְהָיוּ הַדְּבָרִים הָאֵלֶּה, אֲשֶׁר ׀ אָנֹכִי מְצַוְּךָ הַיּוֹם, עַל-לְבָבֶךָ: וְשִׁנַּנְתָּם לְבָנֶיךָ, וְדִבַּרְתָּ בָּם, בְּשִׁבְתְּךָ בְּבֵיתֶךָ, וּבְלֶכְתְּךָ בַדֶּרֶךְ וּבְשָׁכְבְּךָ וּבְקוּמֶךָ: וּקְשַׁרְתָּם לְאוֹת ׀ עַל-יָדֶךָ, וְהָיוּ לְטֹטָפֹת בֵּין ׀ עֵינֶיךָ: וּכְתַבְתָּם ׀ עַל-מְזֻזוֹת בֵּיתֶךָ, וּבִשְׁעָרֶיךָ:

Did You Know??

Our Sages teach us that saying the *Shema* before we go to sleep can protect us during the night while we are sleeping.

When we say the words, "Tie them as a sign upon your arm and let them be between your eyes," we are talking about *tefillin*.

May the angel who saves me from danger bless you. And let them carry my name and the name of my fathers, Avraham and Yitzchak. And may you grow in numbers throughout the land.

הַמַּלְאָךְ הַגֹּאֵל אֹתִי מִכָּל רָע יְבָרֵךְ אֶת הַנְּעָרִים, וְיִקָּרֵא בָהֶם שְׁמִי, וְשֵׁם אֲבֹתַי אַבְרָהָם וְיִצְחָק, וְיִדְגּוּ לָרֹב בְּקֶרֶב הָאָרֶץ.

A Closer Look

We now recite the blessing that Yaakov Avinu gave to his grandchildren, Menasheh and Ephraim, when they were in Egypt.

This prayer, הַמַּלְאָךְ, is really directed toward Hashem, and not to an angel. It is only Hashem Who has the power to save us; no other power can.

סְפִירַת הָעוֹמֶר / Counting the Omer

We start counting the *Omer* on the second night of Pesach, and we continue to count every night until the night before Shavuos.
We recite the *berachah* and then we count the *Omer* (next page).
If we forgot to count one day we count from that day on without reciting the *berachah*.

בָּרוּךְ אַתָּה יהוה אֱלֹהֵינוּ מֶלֶךְ הָעוֹלָם, אֲשֶׁר קִדְּשָׁנוּ בְּמִצְוֹתָיו, וְצִוָּנוּ עַל סְפִירַת הָעוֹמֶר.

Blessed are You, Hashem, our God, King of the universe, Who has made us holy with His mitzvos, and commanded us about the counting of the *Omer*.

A Closer Look

The *Omer* was an offering of the first barley of the year. It was offered up to Hashem in the *Beis HaMikdash* on the second day of Pesach. The Torah commands us to count forty-nine days (seven weeks) from then, and the holiday of Shavuos is celebrated on the fiftieth day. This time period is called "*Sefiras HaOmer* — the Counting of the *Omer*."

Did You Know??
These seven weeks of the Counting of the *Omer* are the same seven weeks when the Jews in the desert prepared themselves to receive the Torah from Hashem at Mount Sinai.

Did You Know??

The period during which we count the *Omer* is a sad time for the Jewish people. The fact that we cannot bring the *Omer* anymore reminds us that we no longer have the *Beis Ha-Mikdash*. Also, during thirty-three days of the *Omer*, 24,000 of Rabbi Akiva's students died. Another bad thing that happened at this time of the year is that, about 800 years ago, during the Crusades, many Jews were murdered.

Day 1

הַיּוֹם יוֹם אֶחָד בָּעוֹמֶר.

Today is one day of the *Omer*.

Day 2

הַיּוֹם שְׁנֵי יָמִים בָּעוֹמֶר.

Today is two days of the *Omer*.

Day 3

הַיּוֹם שְׁלֹשָׁה יָמִים בָּעוֹמֶר.

Today is three days of the *Omer*.

Day 4

הַיּוֹם אַרְבָּעָה יָמִים בָּעוֹמֶר.

Today is four days of the *Omer*.

Day 5

הַיּוֹם חֲמִשָּׁה יָמִים בָּעוֹמֶר.

Today is five days of the *Omer*.

Day 6

הַיּוֹם שִׁשָּׁה יָמִים בָּעוֹמֶר.

Today is six days of the *Omer*.

Day 7

הַיּוֹם שִׁבְעָה יָמִים, שֶׁהֵם שָׁבוּעַ אֶחָד, בָּעוֹמֶר.

Today is seven days, which are one week of the *Omer*.

Day 8

הַיּוֹם שְׁמוֹנָה יָמִים, שֶׁהֵם שָׁבוּעַ אֶחָד וְיוֹם אֶחָד, בָּעוֹמֶר.

Today is eight days, which are one week and one day of the *Omer*.

Day 9

הַיּוֹם תִּשְׁעָה יָמִים, שֶׁהֵם שָׁבוּעַ אֶחָד וּשְׁנֵי יָמִים, בָּעוֹמֶר.

Today is nine days, which are one week and two days of the *Omer*.

Day 10

הַיּוֹם עֲשָׂרָה יָמִים, שֶׁהֵם שָׁבוּעַ אֶחָד וּשְׁלֹשָׁה יָמִים, בָּעוֹמֶר.

Today is ten days, which are one week and three days of the *Omer*.

Day 11

הַיּוֹם אַחַד עָשָׂר יוֹם, שֶׁהֵם שָׁבוּעַ אֶחָד וְאַרְבָּעָה יָמִים, בָּעוֹמֶר.

Today is eleven days, which are one week and four days of the *Omer*.

Day 12

הַיּוֹם שְׁנֵים עָשָׂר יוֹם, שֶׁהֵם שָׁבוּעַ אֶחָד וַחֲמִשָּׁה יָמִים, בָּעוֹמֶר.

Today is twelve days, which are one week and five days of the *Omer*.

Day 13

הַיּוֹם שְׁלֹשָׁה עָשָׂר יוֹם, שֶׁהֵם שָׁבוּעַ אֶחָד וְשִׁשָּׁה יָמִים, בָּעוֹמֶר.

Today is thirteen days, which are one week and six days of the *Omer*.

Day 14

הַיּוֹם אַרְבָּעָה עָשָׂר יוֹם, שֶׁהֵם שְׁנֵי שָׁבוּעוֹת, בָּעוֹמֶר.

Today is fourteen days, which are two weeks of the *Omer*.

Day 15

הַיּוֹם חֲמִשָּׁה עָשָׂר יוֹם, שֶׁהֵם שְׁנֵי שָׁבוּעוֹת וְיוֹם אֶחָד, בָּעוֹמֶר.

Today is fifteen days, which are two weeks and one day of the *Omer*.

Day 16

הַיּוֹם שִׁשָּׁה עָשָׂר יוֹם, שֶׁהֵם שְׁנֵי שָׁבוּעוֹת וּשְׁנֵי יָמִים, בָּעוֹמֶר.

Today is sixteen days, which are two weeks and two days of the *Omer*.

Day 17

הַיּוֹם שִׁבְעָה עָשָׂר יוֹם, שֶׁהֵם שְׁנֵי שָׁבוּעוֹת וּשְׁלֹשָׁה יָמִים, בָּעוֹמֶר.

Today is seventeen days, which are two weeks and three days of the *Omer*.

Day 18

הַיּוֹם שְׁמוֹנָה עָשָׂר יוֹם, שֶׁהֵם שְׁנֵי שָׁבוּעוֹת וְאַרְבָּעָה יָמִים, בָּעוֹמֶר.

Today is eighteen days, which are two weeks and four days of the *Omer*.

Day 19

הַיּוֹם תִּשְׁעָה עָשָׂר יוֹם, שֶׁהֵם שְׁנֵי שָׁבוּעוֹת וַחֲמִשָּׁה יָמִים, בָּעוֹמֶר.

Today is nineteen days, which are two weeks and five days of the *Omer*.

Day 20

הַיּוֹם עֶשְׂרִים יוֹם, שֶׁהֵם שְׁנֵי שָׁבוּעוֹת וְשִׁשָּׁה יָמִים, בָּעוֹמֶר.

Today is twenty days, which are two weeks and six days of the *Omer*.

Day 21

הַיּוֹם אֶחָד וְעֶשְׂרִים יוֹם, שֶׁהֵם שְׁלֹשָׁה שָׁבוּעוֹת, בָּעוֹמֶר.

Today is twenty-one days, which are three weeks of the *Omer*.

Day 22

הַיּוֹם שְׁנַיִם וְעֶשְׂרִים יוֹם, שֶׁהֵם שְׁלֹשָׁה שָׁבוּעוֹת וְיוֹם אֶחָד, בָּעוֹמֶר.

Today is twenty-two days, which are three weeks and one day of the *Omer*.

Day 23

הַיּוֹם שְׁלֹשָׁה וְעֶשְׂרִים יוֹם, שֶׁהֵם שְׁלֹשָׁה שָׁבוּעוֹת וּשְׁנֵי יָמִים, בָּעוֹמֶר.

Today is twenty-three days, which are three weeks and two days of the *Omer*.

Day 24

הַיּוֹם אַרְבָּעָה וְעֶשְׂרִים יוֹם, שֶׁהֵם שְׁלֹשָׁה שָׁבוּעוֹת וּשְׁלֹשָׁה יָמִים, בָּעוֹמֶר.

Today is twenty-four days, which are three weeks and three days of the *Omer*.

Day 25

הַיּוֹם חֲמִשָּׁה וְעֶשְׂרִים יוֹם, שֶׁהֵם שְׁלֹשָׁה שָׁבוּעוֹת וְאַרְבָּעָה יָמִים, בָּעוֹמֶר.

Today is twenty-five days, which are three weeks and four days of the *Omer*.

Day 26

הַיּוֹם שִׁשָּׁה וְעֶשְׂרִים יוֹם, שֶׁהֵם שְׁלֹשָׁה שָׁבוּעוֹת וַחֲמִשָּׁה יָמִים, בָּעוֹמֶר.

Today is twenty-six days, which are three weeks and five days of the *Omer*.

Day 27

הַיּוֹם שִׁבְעָה וְעֶשְׂרִים יוֹם, שֶׁהֵם שְׁלֹשָׁה שָׁבוּעוֹת וְשִׁשָּׁה יָמִים, בָּעוֹמֶר.

Today is twenty-seven days, which are three weeks and six days of the *Omer*.

___ Day 39 ___

הַיּוֹם תִּשְׁעָה וּשְׁלֹשִׁים יוֹם, שֶׁהֵם חֲמִשָּׁה שָׁבוּעוֹת
וְאַרְבָּעָה יָמִים, בָּעוֹמֶר.

Today is thirty-nine days, which are five weeks
and four days of the *Omer.*

___ Day 40 ___

הַיּוֹם אַרְבָּעִים יוֹם, שֶׁהֵם חֲמִשָּׁה שָׁבוּעוֹת
וַחֲמִשָּׁה יָמִים, בָּעוֹמֶר.

Today is forty days, which are five weeks
and five days of the *Omer.*

___ Day 41 ___

הַיּוֹם אֶחָד וְאַרְבָּעִים יוֹם, שֶׁהֵם חֲמִשָּׁה שָׁבוּעוֹת
וְשִׁשָּׁה יָמִים, בָּעוֹמֶר.

Today is forty-one days, which are five weeks
and six days of the *Omer.*

___ Day 42 ___

הַיּוֹם שְׁנַיִם וְאַרְבָּעִים יוֹם, שֶׁהֵם
שִׁשָּׁה שָׁבוּעוֹת, בָּעוֹמֶר.

Today is forty-two days, which are
six weeks of the *Omer.*

___ Day 43 ___

הַיּוֹם שְׁלֹשָׁה וְאַרְבָּעִים יוֹם, שֶׁהֵם שִׁשָּׁה שָׁבוּעוֹת
וְיוֹם אֶחָד, בָּעוֹמֶר.

Today is forty-three days, which are six weeks
and one day of the *Omer.*

___ Day 44 ___

הַיּוֹם אַרְבָּעָה וְאַרְבָּעִים יוֹם, שֶׁהֵם שִׁשָּׁה שָׁבוּעוֹת
וּשְׁנֵי יָמִים, בָּעוֹמֶר.

Today is forty-four days, which are six weeks
and two days of the *Omer.*

___ Day 45 ___

הַיּוֹם חֲמִשָּׁה וְאַרְבָּעִים יוֹם, שֶׁהֵם שִׁשָּׁה שָׁבוּעוֹת
וּשְׁלֹשָׁה יָמִים, בָּעוֹמֶר.

Today is forty-five days, which are six weeks
and three days of the *Omer.*

___ Day 46 ___

הַיּוֹם שִׁשָּׁה וְאַרְבָּעִים יוֹם, שֶׁהֵם שִׁשָּׁה שָׁבוּעוֹת
וְאַרְבָּעָה יָמִים, בָּעוֹמֶר.

Today is forty-six days, which are six weeks
and four days of the *Omer.*

___ Day 47 ___

הַיּוֹם שִׁבְעָה וְאַרְבָּעִים יוֹם, שֶׁהֵם שִׁשָּׁה שָׁבוּעוֹת
וַחֲמִשָּׁה יָמִים, בָּעוֹמֶר.

Today is forty-seven days, which are six weeks
and five days of the *Omer.*

___ Day 48 ___

הַיּוֹם שְׁמוֹנָה וְאַרְבָּעִים יוֹם, שֶׁהֵם שִׁשָּׁה שָׁבוּעוֹת
וְשִׁשָּׁה יָמִים, בָּעוֹמֶר.

Today is forty-eight days, which are six weeks
and six days of the *Omer.*

___ Day 49 ___

הַיּוֹם תִּשְׁעָה וְאַרְבָּעִים יוֹם, שֶׁהֵם
שִׁבְעָה שָׁבוּעוֹת, בָּעוֹמֶר.

Today is forty-nine days, which are
seven weeks of the *Omer.*

___ Day 28 ___

הַיּוֹם שְׁמוֹנָה וְעֶשְׂרִים יוֹם, שֶׁהֵם
אַרְבָּעָה שָׁבוּעוֹת, בָּעוֹמֶר.

Today is twenty-eight days, which are
four weeks of the *Omer.*

___ Day 29 ___

הַיּוֹם תִּשְׁעָה וְעֶשְׂרִים יוֹם, שֶׁהֵם אַרְבָּעָה שָׁבוּעוֹת
וְיוֹם אֶחָד, בָּעוֹמֶר.

Today is twenty-nine days, which are four weeks
and one day of the *Omer.*

___ Day 30 ___

הַיּוֹם שְׁלֹשִׁים יוֹם, שֶׁהֵם אַרְבָּעָה שָׁבוּעוֹת
וּשְׁנֵי יָמִים, בָּעוֹמֶר.

Today is thirty days, which are four weeks
and two days of the *Omer.*

___ Day 31 ___

הַיּוֹם אֶחָד וּשְׁלֹשִׁים יוֹם, שֶׁהֵם אַרְבָּעָה שָׁבוּעוֹת
וּשְׁלֹשָׁה יָמִים, בָּעוֹמֶר.

Today is thirty-one days, which are four weeks
and three days of the *Omer.*

___ Day 32 ___

הַיּוֹם שְׁנַיִם וּשְׁלֹשִׁים יוֹם, שֶׁהֵם אַרְבָּעָה שָׁבוּעוֹת
וְאַרְבָּעָה יָמִים, בָּעוֹמֶר.

Today is thirty-two days, which are four weeks
and four days of the *Omer.*

___ Day 33 ___

הַיּוֹם שְׁלֹשָׁה וּשְׁלֹשִׁים יוֹם, שֶׁהֵם אַרְבָּעָה שָׁבוּעוֹת
וַחֲמִשָּׁה יָמִים, בָּעוֹמֶר.

Today is thirty-three days, which are four weeks
and five days of the *Omer.*

___ Day 34 ___

הַיּוֹם אַרְבָּעָה וּשְׁלֹשִׁים יוֹם, שֶׁהֵם אַרְבָּעָה שָׁבוּעוֹת
וְשִׁשָּׁה יָמִים, בָּעוֹמֶר.

Today is thirty-four days, which are four weeks
and six days of the *Omer.*

___ Day 35 ___

הַיּוֹם חֲמִשָּׁה וּשְׁלֹשִׁים יוֹם, שֶׁהֵם
חֲמִשָּׁה שָׁבוּעוֹת, בָּעוֹמֶר.

Today is thirty-five days, which are
five weeks of the *Omer.*

___ Day 36 ___

הַיּוֹם שִׁשָּׁה וּשְׁלֹשִׁים יוֹם, שֶׁהֵם חֲמִשָּׁה שָׁבוּעוֹת
וְיוֹם אֶחָד, בָּעוֹמֶר.

Today is thirty-six days, which are five weeks
and one day of the *Omer.*

___ Day 37 ___

הַיּוֹם שִׁבְעָה וּשְׁלֹשִׁים יוֹם, שֶׁהֵם חֲמִשָּׁה שָׁבוּעוֹת
וּשְׁנֵי יָמִים, בָּעוֹמֶר.

Today is thirty-seven days, which are five weeks
and two days of the *Omer.*

___ Day 38 ___

הַיּוֹם שְׁמוֹנָה וּשְׁלֹשִׁים יוֹם, שֶׁהֵם חֲמִשָּׁה שָׁבוּעוֹת
וּשְׁלֹשָׁה יָמִים, בָּעוֹמֶר.

Today is thirty-eight days, which are five weeks
and three days of the *Omer.*

הַדְלָקַת נֵרוֹת / Candle Lighting

Before Shabbos starts, we light the candles and say this *berachah*:

Blessed are You, Hashem, our God, King of the universe, Who has made us holy with His mitzvos, and commanded us to light the Shabbos candle.

בָּרוּךְ אַתָּה יהוה אֱלֹהֵינוּ מֶלֶךְ הָעוֹלָם, אֲשֶׁר קִדְּשָׁנוּ בְּמִצְוֹתָיו, וְצִוָּנוּ לְהַדְלִיק נֵר שֶׁל שַׁבָּת.

Before Yom Tov starts, we light the candles and say this *berachah*
(when Yom Tov comes out on Shabbos we add the words in parentheses):

Blessed are You, Hashem, our God, King of the universe, Who has made us holy with His mitzvos, and commanded us to light the (Shabbos candle and the) Yom Tov candle.

בָּרוּךְ אַתָּה יהוה אֱלֹהֵינוּ מֶלֶךְ הָעוֹלָם, אֲשֶׁר קִדְּשָׁנוּ בְּמִצְוֹתָיו, וְצִוָּנוּ לְהַדְלִיק נֵר שֶׁל (שַׁבָּת וְשֶׁל) יוֹם טוֹב.

On Yom Tov we also add the following *berachah*:

Blessed are You, Hashem, our God, King of the universe, for keeping us alive, taking care of us, and bringing us to this time.

בָּרוּךְ אַתָּה יהוה אֱלֹהֵינוּ מֶלֶךְ הָעוֹלָם, שֶׁהֶחֱיָנוּ וְקִיְּמָנוּ וְהִגִּיעָנוּ לַזְּמַן הַזֶּה.

A Closer Look
After a woman lights the candles, she waves her hands over the lights. This is a time when a woman has a special connection to Hashem, and therefore a good time for her to pray for something that she wants.

קַבָּלַת שַׁבָּת / Kabbalas Shabbos

We sing *Lechah Dodi* in shul every Friday night. We compare Shabbos to a *kallah* (bride) that is married to the Jewish people. The same way a *chasan* (groom) looks forward to welcoming his new bride, we look forward to welcoming our bride, the Shabbos, each and every week.

Come to greet the holy Shabbos bride,
let us welcome the Shabbos.

> Come to greet the holy Shabbos bride,
> let us welcome the Shabbos.

The words "Keep Shabbos" and "Remember
the Shabbos" in the Ten Commandments
were both said together;
God made us hear both words at the same time.
Hashem is One and His Name is One,
so that all should praise Him.

> Come to greet the holy Shabbos bride,
> let us welcome the Shabbos.

Come let us go and welcome the Shabbos,
for Shabbos is the source of all blessings.
From the beginning, and from ancient times,
the Shabbos was honored.
It was the last thing Hashem created,
but the first thing He thought of.

> Come to greet the holy Shabbos bride,
> let us welcome the Shabbos.

The *Beis HaMikdash* of the King
and the royal city Jerusalem,
come, arise from being destroyed!
Too long have all of you
been sad and filled with tears.
Hashem will take pity on you.

> Come to greet the holy Shabbos bride,
> let us welcome the Shabbos.

Shake yourself off from the dust and get up.
Put on your beautiful clothing, My people,
through Mashiach the son of Yishai
from Bethlehem.
Hashem, come close to my soul and redeem it.

> Come to greet the holy Shabbos bride,
> let us welcome the Shabbos.

לְכָה דוֹדִי לִקְרַאת כַּלָּה,
פְּנֵי שַׁבָּת נְקַבְּלָה.
לְכָה דוֹדִי לִקְרַאת כַּלָּה, פְּנֵי שַׁבָּת נְקַבְּלָה.

שָׁמוֹר וְזָכוֹר בְּדִבּוּר אֶחָד,
הִשְׁמִיעָנוּ אֵל הַמְּיֻחָד,
יהוה אֶחָד וּשְׁמוֹ אֶחָד,
לְשֵׁם וּלְתִפְאֶרֶת וְלִתְהִלָּה.
לְכָה דוֹדִי לִקְרַאת כַּלָּה, פְּנֵי שַׁבָּת נְקַבְּלָה.

לִקְרַאת שַׁבָּת לְכוּ וְנֵלְכָה,
כִּי הִיא מְקוֹר הַבְּרָכָה,
מֵרֹאשׁ מִקֶּדֶם נְסוּכָה,
סוֹף מַעֲשֶׂה בְּמַחֲשָׁבָה תְּחִלָּה.
לְכָה דוֹדִי לִקְרַאת כַּלָּה, פְּנֵי שַׁבָּת נְקַבְּלָה.

מִקְדַּשׁ מֶלֶךְ עִיר מְלוּכָה,
קוּמִי צְאִי מִתּוֹךְ הַהֲפֵכָה,
רַב לָךְ שֶׁבֶת בְּעֵמֶק הַבָּכָא,
וְהוּא יַחֲמוֹל עָלַיִךְ חֶמְלָה.
לְכָה דוֹדִי לִקְרַאת כַּלָּה, פְּנֵי שַׁבָּת נְקַבְּלָה.

הִתְנַעֲרִי מֵעָפָר קוּמִי,
לִבְשִׁי בִּגְדֵי תִפְאַרְתֵּךְ עַמִּי,
עַל יַד בֶּן יִשַׁי בֵּית הַלַּחְמִי,
קָרְבָה אֶל נַפְשִׁי גְאָלָהּ.
לְכָה דוֹדִי לִקְרַאת כַּלָּה, פְּנֵי שַׁבָּת נְקַבְּלָה.

Did You Know??
The name of the author of this song, Shlomo HaLevi, is hidden somewhere in the Hebrew words. Can you find his name?

Did You Know??
Many sages would go out to the field as the time for Shabbos was drawing near. Then they would sing *Lechah Dodi* and welcome the Shabbos, just as they would go to greet an important royal guest.

Wake up! Wake up!
It is time that Your light should shine.
Wake up, wake up,
    and sing a song of praise to Hashem.
The glory of Hashem shall be shown to you.
        Come to greet the holy Shabbos bride,
          let us welcome the Shabbos.

Don't be ashamed, My people,
    don't be embarrassed.
Why are you sad? Why are you upset?
Poor people will find shelter in you,
    as Jerusalem will be built on its hilltop.
        Come to greet the holy Shabbos bride,
          let us welcome the Shabbos.

Let anyone who wants to do evil to you
    be destroyed.
And may those who tried to kill you
    be chased away.
Hashem will be happy with you,
    the same way a groom is happy with his bride.
        Come to greet the holy Shabbos bride,
          let us welcome the Shabbos.

You will be numerous and spread out
    to the right and to the left,
    and you will praise Hashem.
The Mashiach, who descends
    from Yehudah's son Peretz, will come,
    and we will all be happy and joyous.
        Come to greet the holy Shabbos bride,
          let us welcome the Shabbos.

הִתְעוֹרְרִי הִתְעוֹרְרִי,

כִּי בָא אוֹרֵךְ קוּמִי אוֹרִי,

עוּרִי עוּרִי שִׁיר דַּבֵּרִי,

כְּבוֹד יהוה עָלַיִךְ נִגְלָה.

לְכָה דוֹדִי לִקְרַאת כַּלָּה, פְּנֵי שַׁבָּת נְקַבְּלָה.

לֹא תֵבוֹשִׁי וְלֹא תִכָּלְמִי,

מַה תִּשְׁתּוֹחֲחִי וּמַה תֶּהֱמִי,

בָּךְ יֶחֱסוּ עֲנִיֵּי עַמִּי,

וְנִבְנְתָה עִיר עַל תִּלָּהּ.

לְכָה דוֹדִי לִקְרַאת כַּלָּה, פְּנֵי שַׁבָּת נְקַבְּלָה.

וְהָיוּ לִמְשִׁסָּה שֹׁאסָיִךְ,

וְרָחֲקוּ כָּל מְבַלְּעָיִךְ,

יָשִׂישׂ עָלַיִךְ אֱלֹהָיִךְ,

כִּמְשׂוֹשׂ חָתָן עַל כַּלָּה.

לְכָה דוֹדִי לִקְרַאת כַּלָּה, פְּנֵי שַׁבָּת נְקַבְּלָה.

יָמִין וּשְׂמֹאל תִּפְרוֹצִי.

וְאֶת יהוה תַּעֲרִיצִי,

עַל יַד אִישׁ בֶּן פַּרְצִי,

וְנִשְׂמְחָה וְנָגִילָה.

לְכָה דוֹדִי לִקְרַאת כַּלָּה, פְּנֵי שַׁבָּת נְקַבְּלָה.

A Closer Look
   Hashem created Shabbos on the seventh day as a day of rest, and filled it with His holiness. Since that first Shabbos, almost 6,000 years ago, every seventh day has received that special holiness directly from Hashem. Shabbos is not dependent on us to give it its holiness; it received its holiness directly from Hashem when He made the world. By keeping the laws of Shabbos we build on that holiness every week and make it even greater.
   The exact days of the Jewish holidays, on the other hand, are determined by man, because the Jewish court decides when Rosh Chodesh, the beginning of each new month, will be.

Everyone now stands and faces the back of the shul to greet the Shabbos Bride.
When we say בּוֹאִי כַלָּה, we bow and turn toward the front of the shul
to show that the Shabbos Bride has come.

Come in peace, crown of the Jewish people.
Come in happiness and joy.
Stay among the Jewish people,
Come in, Shabbos Bride!
Come in, Shabbos Bride!
Come to greet the holy Shabbos bride,
let us welcome the Shabbos.

בּוֹאִי בְשָׁלוֹם עֲטֶרֶת בַּעְלָה,

גַּם בְּשִׂמְחָה וּבְצָהֳלָה,

תּוֹךְ אֱמוּנֵי עַם סְגֻלָּה,

בּוֹאִי כַלָּה, בּוֹאִי כַלָּה.

לְכָה דוֹדִי לִקְרַאת כַּלָּה, פְּנֵי שַׁבָּת נְקַבְּלָה.

Mizmor Shir / מִזְמוֹר שִׁיר

A song for the Shabbos day. It is good to thank Hashem and praise Him. We talk in the morning about how kind You are, and at night we speak of our faith in You. We sing Your praises with musical instruments. You have made me happy, Hashem, with what You have done; and because of all You have made, I sing happy songs. A foolish person cannot understand Your ways — that a wicked person will sometimes succeed, so they can in the end be brought down by You and destroyed. But You remain great forever. Your enemies will die, and whoever does evil will be sent away. My eyes have seen my enemies come against me, My ears have heard that they will be destroyed. A *tzaddik* will grow like a date tree; he will grow strong in Your ways like a cedar tree. They will be in the *Beis HaMidkash,* and grow in Your courtyards. Even in their old age, they will still be fresh and strong, and tell everyone that Hashem is righteous, and He does nothing unjust.

מִזְמוֹר שִׁיר לְיוֹם הַשַּׁבָּת. טוֹב לְהֹדוֹת לַיהוה, וּלְזַמֵּר לְשִׁמְךָ עֶלְיוֹן. לְהַגִּיד בַּבֹּקֶר חַסְדֶּךָ, וֶאֱמוּנָתְךָ בַּלֵּילוֹת. עֲלֵי עָשׂוֹר וַעֲלֵי נָבֶל, עֲלֵי הִגָּיוֹן בְּכִנּוֹר. כִּי שִׂמַּחְתַּנִי יהוה בְּפָעֳלֶךָ, בְּמַעֲשֵׂי יָדֶיךָ אֲרַנֵּן. מַה גָּדְלוּ מַעֲשֶׂיךָ יהוה, מְאֹד עָמְקוּ מַחְשְׁבֹתֶיךָ. אִישׁ בַּעַר לֹא יֵדָע, וּכְסִיל לֹא יָבִין אֶת זֹאת. בִּפְרֹחַ רְשָׁעִים כְּמוֹ עֵשֶׂב, וַיָּצִיצוּ כָּל פֹּעֲלֵי אָוֶן, לְהִשָּׁמְדָם עֲדֵי עַד. וְאַתָּה מָרוֹם לְעֹלָם יהוה. כִּי הִנֵּה אֹיְבֶיךָ, יהוה, כִּי הִנֵּה אֹיְבֶיךָ יֹאבֵדוּ, יִתְפָּרְדוּ כָּל פֹּעֲלֵי אָוֶן. וַתָּרֶם כִּרְאֵים קַרְנִי, בַּלֹּתִי בְּשֶׁמֶן רַעֲנָן. וַתַּבֵּט עֵינִי בְּשׁוּרָי, בַּקָּמִים עָלַי מְרֵעִים, תִּשְׁמַעְנָה אָזְנָי. צַדִּיק כַּתָּמָר יִפְרָח, כְּאֶרֶז בַּלְּבָנוֹן יִשְׂגֶּה. שְׁתוּלִים בְּבֵית יהוה, בְּחַצְרוֹת אֱלֹהֵינוּ יַפְרִיחוּ. עוֹד יְנוּבוּן בְּשֵׂיבָה, דְּשֵׁנִים וְרַעֲנַנִּים יִהְיוּ. לְהַגִּיד כִּי יָשָׁר יהוה, צוּרִי וְלֹא עַוְלָתָה בּוֹ.

A Closer Look
This is the psalm that the *Leviim* sang in the *Beis HaMikdash* every Shabbos when the morning sacrifices were brought.

Did You Know??
The moment we say *Mizmor Shir L'yom HaShabbos,* we accept upon ourselves the holiness of Shabbos.

Some say the holiness of Shabbos starts from the moment we say ''Come in, Shabbos Bride,'' in לְכָה דוֹדִי.

בִּרְכַּת הַבָּנִים / Blessing the Children

Some people have the custom that the father blesses his children when he returns home from shul on Friday night.

FOR A BOY:

יְשִׂמְךָ אֱלֹהִים כְּאֶפְרַיִם וְכִמְנַשֶּׁה.

May Hashem make you just like Ephraim and Menasheh
(the grandchildren of Yaakov Avinu).

FOR A GIRL:

יְשִׂמֵךְ אֱלֹהִים כְּשָׂרָה רִבְקָה רָחֵל וְלֵאָה.

May Hashem make you just like Sarah, Rivkah, Rachel, and Leah
(the four mothers).

FOR BOTH:

יְבָרֶכְךָ יהוה וְיִשְׁמְרֶךָ. יָאֵר יהוה פָּנָיו אֵלֶיךָ וִיחֻנֶּךָּ.
יִשָּׂא יהוה פָּנָיו אֵלֶיךָ, וְיָשֵׂם לְךָ שָׁלוֹם.

May Hashem bless you and watch over you. May the Light of Hashem shine upon you.
May Hashem look favorably on you, and bring you peace.

Did You Know??

This blessing for boys is the same blessing that Yaakov gave to his grandchildren, Ephraim and Menasheh. Even though they were both raised in the palace of Pharaoh, the two still grew up to be good and holy Jewish men. Yaakov, himself, recommended that parents bless their children with this *berachah*.

It is the wish of all Jewish parents that they have good and holy daughters, similar to Sarah, Rivkah, Rachel, and Leah.

A Closer Look

Because of its holiness, Shabbos is an excellent time to give blessings. One of the most important blessings is to have good and righteous children. The parent places both hands upon the child's head and blesses him or her.

78

שָׁלוֹם עֲלֵיכֶם / *Shalom Aleichem*

Two angels enter our house with us as we return home from shul. The whole family then sings *Shalom Aleichem*.
Each stanza is said three times.

Come in peace,
  holy angels of Hashem,
    angels of the King Who rules over all kings.

May you come into my house in peace,
  angels of peace,
    angels of the King Who rules over all kings.

Bless me with peace,
  angels of peace,
    angels of the King Who rules over all kings.

May you also leave in peace,
  angels of peace,
    angels of the King Who rules over all kings.

שָׁלוֹם עֲלֵיכֶם,
מַלְאֲכֵי הַשָּׁרֵת, מַלְאֲכֵי עֶלְיוֹן,
מִמֶּלֶךְ מַלְכֵי הַמְּלָכִים
הַקָּדוֹשׁ בָּרוּךְ הוּא.

בּוֹאֲכֶם לְשָׁלוֹם,
מַלְאֲכֵי הַשָּׁלוֹם, מַלְאֲכֵי עֶלְיוֹן,
מִמֶּלֶךְ מַלְכֵי הַמְּלָכִים
הַקָּדוֹשׁ בָּרוּךְ הוּא.

בָּרְכוּנִי לְשָׁלוֹם,
מַלְאֲכֵי הַשָּׁלוֹם, מַלְאֲכֵי עֶלְיוֹן,
מִמֶּלֶךְ מַלְכֵי הַמְּלָכִים
הַקָּדוֹשׁ בָּרוּךְ הוּא.

צֵאתְכֶם לְשָׁלוֹם,
מַלְאֲכֵי הַשָּׁלוֹם, מַלְאֲכֵי עֶלְיוֹן,
מִמֶּלֶךְ מַלְכֵי הַמְּלָכִים
הַקָּדוֹשׁ בָּרוּךְ הוּא.

Did You Know??
    Our Sages teach us that we come home from shul on Friday night with two angels — a good angel and a bad angel. If the Shabbos candles are lit and the Shabbos table is set and ready for the family, the good angel says, "May it be like this again next Shabbos," and the bad angel must answer "Amen." If, on the other hand, the house is filled with people not keeping the Shabbos, the bad angel says, "May it be like this again next Shabbos," and the good angel must answer "Amen."

A Closer Look

Just as Shabbos is a holy day to Hashem, and He stopped working on Shabbos, we also make Shabbos into a day of holiness and rest. On Shabbos we stop working and we try to improve our spiritual life. We learn Torah, we rest, we rejoice, and we thank Hashem for all He does for us.

קִדּוּש / *Friday Night Kiddush*

The father says *Kiddush*. In some families, everyone listens and answers "Amen" at the end of *Kiddush*. In other families, everyone says *Kiddush* quietly along with the father. In still others, each person says *Kiddush* separately out loud.

Quietly: And it was evening and it was morning —

וַיְהִי עֶרֶב וַיְהִי בֹקֶר — Quietly

The sixth day of creation.

And the heavens, the earth, and all that is in them were finished. On the seventh day, Hashem stopped His work that He had been doing, and He rested on the seventh day from all His work. And Hashem blessed the seventh day and made it holy, because on that day He rested from all His work that He had created.

יוֹם הַשִּׁשִּׁי. וַיְכֻלּוּ הַשָּׁמַיִם וְהָאָרֶץ וְכָל צְבָאָם. וַיְכַל אֱלֹהִים בַּיּוֹם הַשְּׁבִיעִי מְלַאכְתּוֹ אֲשֶׁר עָשָׂה, וַיִּשְׁבֹּת בַּיּוֹם הַשְּׁבִיעִי מִכָּל מְלַאכְתּוֹ אֲשֶׁר עָשָׂה. וַיְבָרֶךְ אֱלֹהִים אֶת יוֹם הַשְּׁבִיעִי וַיְקַדֵּשׁ אֹתוֹ, כִּי בוֹ שָׁבַת מִכָּל מְלַאכְתּוֹ אֲשֶׁר בָּרָא אֱלֹהִים לַעֲשׂוֹת.

Please listen my masters:

סַבְרִי מָרָנָן וְרַבָּנָן וְרַבּוֹתַי:

Blessed are You, Hashem, our God, King of the universe, Who has created the fruit of the grapevine.

בָּרוּךְ אַתָּה יהוה אֱלֹהֵינוּ מֶלֶךְ הָעוֹלָם, בּוֹרֵא פְּרִי הַגָּפֶן.

Whoever is not saying *Kiddush* answers "Amen."

Blessed are You, Hashem, our God, King of the universe, Who made us holy with his mitzvos, and wanted us to be His people, and because of His great love for us, gave us the Shabbos, to remind us that it was He Who created the world. Shabbos is the head of all Holy Days. And Shabbos also reminds us that Hashem took us out of Egypt. You chose us from among the rest of the nations. And it is us that You made holy from among all the other nations. And with great love You gave us the holy Shabbos. Blessed are You, Hashem, Who makes Shabbos holy.

בָּרוּךְ אַתָּה יהוה אֱלֹהֵינוּ מֶלֶךְ הָעוֹלָם, אֲשֶׁר קִדְּשָׁנוּ בְּמִצְוֹתָיו וְרָצָה בָנוּ, וְשַׁבַּת קָדְשׁוֹ בְּאַהֲבָה וּבְרָצוֹן הִנְחִילָנוּ, זִכָּרוֹן לְמַעֲשֵׂה בְרֵאשִׁית. כִּי הוּא יוֹם תְּחִלָּה לְמִקְרָאֵי קֹדֶשׁ, זֵכֶר לִיצִיאַת מִצְרָיִם. כִּי בָנוּ בָחַרְתָּ, וְאוֹתָנוּ קִדַּשְׁתָּ, מִכָּל הָעַמִּים. וְשַׁבַּת קָדְשְׁךָ בְּאַהֲבָה וּבְרָצוֹן הִנְחַלְתָּנוּ. בָּרוּךְ אַתָּה יהוה, מְקַדֵּשׁ הַשַּׁבָּת.

Whoever is not saying *Kiddush* answers "Amen."

Did You Know??
Shabbos is the holiest day of the Jewish year — even holier than Rosh Hashanah and Yom Kippur!
If all Jews would keep two Shabbasos in a row, the Mashiach would come.

A Closer Look
Shabbos is a sign between Hashem and the Jewish people that it is He Who created everything. When we observe the Shabbos, it shows that we believe that Hashem created the world and rested on the seventh day.

זְמִירוֹת / Shabbos Zemiros

On Friday night the entire family sits together around the Shabbos table. We share thoughts on the Torah and we sing *zemiros*. The most beautiful part of the week is when the whole family is together, celebrating their love of Hashem and of each other.

יָה רִבּוֹן / YAH RIBON

Master of all the worlds,
   You are the King, King of all kings.
We love to tell about
   the wonderful things You do.
Master of all the worlds,
   You are the King, King of all kings.

I will think about how to praise You,
   day and night,
   You are Hashem,
   Creator of everything that lives,
   holy angels and humans,
   animals and birds.
> Master of all the worlds,
> You are the King, King of all kings.

Your deeds are great and mighty,
   putting down the arrogant,
   and straightening up
   those who are bent down.
Even if we lived thousands of years,
   we would never fully understand
   even a little bit of what You can do.
> Master of all the worlds,
> You are the King, King of all kings.

You, Hashem, Who deserve to be honored,
   save the Jewish people from their enemies
   and bring Your people out of their sad exile,
   the Jewish people,
   whom You chose from all the other nations.
> Master of all the worlds,
> You are the King, King of all kings.

Return to the *Beis HaMikdash,*
   return to the Holy of Holies,
   the place where everyone is happy and joyous.
They will sing songs of praise to You
   in Jerusalem, the holy city of beauty.
> Master of all the worlds,
> You are the King, King of all kings.

יָה רִבּוֹן עָלַם וְעָלְמַיָּא,
אַנְתְּ הוּא מַלְכָּא מֶלֶךְ מַלְכַיָּא,
עוֹבַד גְּבוּרְתֵּךְ וְתִמְהַיָּא,
שְׁפַר קֳדָמָךְ לְהַחֲוַיָּא.

יָה רִבּוֹן עָלַם וְעָלְמַיָּא,
אַנְתְּ הוּא מַלְכָּא מֶלֶךְ מַלְכַיָּא.

שְׁבָחִין אֲסַדֵּר צַפְרָא וְרַמְשָׁא,
לָךְ אֱלָהָא קַדִּישָׁא דִּי בְרָא כָל נַפְשָׁא,
עִירִין קַדִּישִׁין וּבְנֵי אֱנָשָׁא,
חֵיוַת בָּרָא וְעוֹפֵי שְׁמַיָּא.

יָה רִבּוֹן עָלַם וְעָלְמַיָּא,
אַנְתְּ הוּא מַלְכָּא מֶלֶךְ מַלְכַיָּא.

רַבְרְבִין עוֹבְדֵיךְ וְתַקִּיפִין,
מָכִיךְ רְמַיָּא וְזַקִּיף כְּפִיפִין,
לוּ יִחְיֶה גְבַר שְׁנִין אַלְפִין,
לָא יֵעוֹל גְּבוּרְתֵּךְ בְּחֻשְׁבְּנַיָּא.

יָה רִבּוֹן עָלַם וְעָלְמַיָּא,
אַנְתְּ הוּא מַלְכָּא מֶלֶךְ מַלְכַיָּא.

אֱלָהָא דִּי לֵהּ יְקַר וּרְבוּתָא,
פְּרוֹק יַת עָנָךְ מִפּוּם אַרְיָוָתָא,
וְאַפֵּיק יַת עַמֵּךְ מִגּוֹ גָלוּתָא,
עַמֵּךְ דִּי בְחַרְתְּ מִכָּל אֻמַּיָּא.

יָה רִבּוֹן עָלַם וְעָלְמַיָּא,
אַנְתְּ הוּא מַלְכָּא מֶלֶךְ מַלְכַיָּא.

לְמִקְדָּשֵׁךְ תּוּב וּלְקֹדֶשׁ קֻדְשִׁין,
אֲתַר דִּי בֵהּ יֶחֱדוּן רוּחִין וְנַפְשִׁין,
וִיזַמְּרוּן לָךְ שִׁירִין וְרַחֲשִׁין,
בִּירוּשְׁלֵם קַרְתָּא דְשׁוּפְרַיָּא.

יָה רִבּוֹן עָלַם וְעָלְמַיָּא,
אַנְתְּ הוּא מַלְכָּא מֶלֶךְ מַלְכַיָּא.

Did You Know??
   There is no mention at all of Shabbos in *Kah Ribon.* But it is a beautiful song, filled with praise and love for Hashem and His love for us. It has therefore become one of the most popular Shabbos *zemiros* that we sing.
   The first letters of these five stanzas in Hebrew spell the name of the author of *Kah Ribon.* Can you figure out his name?

A Closer Look
   The beauty and the holiness of Shabbos give us a small taste of the World to Come.
   On Shabbos it is not only we who sing *zemiros,* but if we listen very closely, we can hear the Shabbos, itself, singing.

צוּר מִשֶּׁלּוֹ / TZUR MISHELO

The following song is an introduction to *Bircas HaMazon*.
We invite all guests to come join us and thank Hashem for all the delicious food He has given us.

Hashem, the Rock of strength,
Whose food we have eaten —
come bless Him, my good friends.
For we have had enough to eat,
and even left some over,
just as Hashem wants.

He feeds the whole world,
our Shepherd, our Father.
We have eaten His bread,
and drunk His wine; therefore,
let us thank Him and praise Him.
Let us sing out loud,
there is nothing as holy as Hashem.

Hashem, the Rock of strength, Whose food we have
eaten — come bless Him, my good friends.
For we have had enough to eat,
and even left some over, just as Hashem wants.

צוּר מִשֶּׁלּוֹ אָכַלְנוּ
בָּרְכוּ אֱמוּנַי,
שָׂבַעְנוּ וְהוֹתַרְנוּ כִּדְבַר יהוה.

הַזָּן אֶת עוֹלָמוֹ רוֹעֵנוּ אָבִינוּ,
אָכַלְנוּ אֶת לַחְמוֹ וְיֵינוֹ שָׁתִינוּ,
עַל כֵּן נוֹדֶה לִשְׁמוֹ וּנְהַלְלוֹ בְּפִינוּ,
אָמַרְנוּ וְעָנִינוּ אֵין קָדוֹשׁ כַּיהוה.

צוּר מִשֶּׁלּוֹ אָכַלְנוּ בָּרְכוּ אֱמוּנַי,
שָׂבַעְנוּ וְהוֹתַרְנוּ כִּדְבַר יהוה.

A Closer Look
Shabbos is a gift that Hashem has given to the Jewish people. Hashem is happy when we appreciate His precious gift.

With song and thanks we bless Hashem
for the wonderful and good land
that He gave our fathers;
with food He satisfied our souls.
His kindness covers us;
Hashem is always true.

Hashem, the Rock of strength, Whose food we have
eaten — come bless Him, my good friends.
For we have had enough to eat,
and even left some over, just as Hashem wants.

בְּשִׁיר וְקוֹל תּוֹדָה נְבָרֵךְ אֱלֹהֵינוּ,
עַל אֶרֶץ חֶמְדָּה טוֹבָה
שֶׁהִנְחִיל לַאֲבוֹתֵינוּ,
מָזוֹן וְצֵדָה הִשְׂבִּיעַ לְנַפְשֵׁנוּ,
חַסְדּוֹ גָּבַר עָלֵינוּ וֶאֱמֶת יהוה.

צוּר מִשֶּׁלּוֹ אָכַלְנוּ בָּרְכוּ אֱמוּנַי,
שָׂבַעְנוּ וְהוֹתַרְנוּ כִּדְבַר יהוה.

Have mercy on us with Your kindness,
upon Your people,
on Zion where Your Presence rests,
the home of our glory.
Mashiach, the descendant of King David
Your servant, will come and save us —
Hashem's Mashiach is our breath of life.

Hashem, the Rock of strength, Whose food we have
eaten — come bless Him, my good friends.
For we have had enough to eat,
and even left some over, just as Hashem wants.

May the *Beis HaMikdash* be rebuilt,
may Jerusalem be filled again.
We will sing a new song there,
and go up to Jerusalem
with a happy song.
May Hashem, the holy and merciful God,
be blessed,
over a full cup of wine,
with which He has blessed us.

Hashem, the Rock of strength, Whose food we have
eaten — come bless Him, my good friends.
For we have had enough to eat,
and even left some over, just as Hashem wants.

רַחֵם בְּחַסְדֶּךָ עַל עַמְּךָ צוּרֵנוּ,
עַל צִיּוֹן מִשְׁכַּן כְּבוֹדֶךָ
זְבוּל בֵּית תִּפְאַרְתֵּנוּ,
בֶּן דָּוִד עַבְדֶּךָ יָבֹא וְיִגְאָלֵנוּ,
רוּחַ אַפֵּינוּ מְשִׁיחַ יהוה.

צוּר מִשֶּׁלוֹ אָכַלְנוּ בָּרְכוּ אֱמוּנַי,
שָׂבַעְנוּ וְהוֹתַרְנוּ כִּדְבַר יהוה.

יִבָּנֶה הַמִּקְדָּשׁ עִיר צִיּוֹן תְּמַלֵּא,
וְשָׁם נָשִׁיר שִׁיר חָדָשׁ
וּבִרְנָנָה נַעֲלֶה,
הָרַחֲמָן הַנִּקְדָּשׁ יִתְבָּרַךְ וְיִתְעַלֶּה,
עַל כּוֹס יַיִן מָלֵא כְּבִרְכַּת יהוה.

צוּר מִשֶּׁלוֹ אָכַלְנוּ בָּרְכוּ אֱמוּנַי,
שָׂבַעְנוּ וְהוֹתַרְנוּ כִּדְבַר יהוה.

Did You Know??
When Hashem created the world He gave each day a partner. Sunday was given Monday, Tuesday was given Wednesday, and Thursday was given Friday. "Only I have no partner," Shabbos complained to Hashem. Hashem answered, "The Jewish people will be your partner." From then on Shabbos and the Jewish people have always been connected. One can never be separated from the other. As long as the Jewish people guard the Shabbos, the Shabbos guards the Jewish people.

יוֹם זֶה מְכֻבָּד / YOM ZEH MECHUBAD

This song is generally sung during the day on Shabbos.
It teaches us that whoever honors the Shabbos will be greatly rewarded by Hashem.

This day, Shabbos,
  is more honored than all the other days,
because on this day Hashem rested.

For six days you shall do all your work,
  but the seventh day is for Hashem.
On Shabbos you should not work,
  because Hashem completed all His work
  in six days.

This day, Shabbos,
  is more honored than all the other days,
  because on this day Hashem rested.

יוֹם זֶה מְכֻבָּד מִכָּל יָמִים,
כִּי בוֹ שָׁבַת צוּר עוֹלָמִים.

שֵׁשֶׁת יָמִים תַּעֲשֶׂה מְלַאכְתֶּךָ,
וְיוֹם הַשְּׁבִיעִי לֵאלֹהֶיךָ,
שַׁבָּת לֹא תַעֲשֶׂה בוֹ מְלָאכָה,
כִּי כֹל עָשָׂה שֵׁשֶׁת יָמִים.

יוֹם זֶה מְכֻבָּד מִכָּל יָמִים,
כִּי בוֹ שָׁבַת צוּר עוֹלָמִים.

Shabbos is first among the holidays,
  it is a day of rest, the holy Shabbos.
Let everyone say *Kiddush* on his wine,
  and have two whole challos.

This day, Shabbos,
  is more honored than all the other days,
  because on this day Hashem rested.

רִאשׁוֹן הוּא לְמִקְרָאֵי קֹדֶשׁ,
יוֹם שַׁבָּתוֹן יוֹם שַׁבַּת קֹדֶשׁ,
עַל כֵּן כָּל אִישׁ בְּיֵינוֹ יְקַדֵּשׁ,
עַל שְׁתֵּי לֶחֶם יִבְצְעוּ תְמִימִים.

יוֹם זֶה מְכֻבָּד מִכָּל יָמִים,
כִּי בוֹ שָׁבַת צוּר עוֹלָמִים.

Did You Know??
The first letters of the five stanzas in Hebrew spell out the name of the author of *Yom Zeh Mechubad.* Can you figure out his name?
On Shabbos, Hashem gives each of us an extra *neshamah* (soul) that brings us closer to Him.

A Closer Look
When we sing *zemiros,* our soul sings out to Hashem, and we feel a special type of pleasure and joy.

Eat delicious foods, enjoy sweet drinks,
  because Hashem will give
  to all who are close to Him
clothes to wear and enough food,
meat and fish and everything else tasty.
        This day, Shabbos,
    is more honored than all the other days,
    because on this day Hashem rested.

You will not lack anything,
  you will eat and be satisfied,
  and bless Hashem, Whom you love,
  because He has blessed the Jewish people,
  more than any other nation.
        This day, Shabbos,
    is more honored than all the other days,
    because on this day Hashem rested.

The heavens talk of Hashem's glory,
  and the earth is full of His kindness.
Look at all the things He has done,
  for He is the One
  Who makes everything perfectly.
        This day, Shabbos,
    is more honored than all the other days,
    because on this day Hashem rested.

אֱכוֹל מַשְׁמַנִּים שְׁתֵה מַמְתַּקִּים,
כִּי אֵל יִתֵּן לְכָל בּוֹ דְבֵקִים,
בֶּגֶד לִלְבּוֹשׁ לֶחֶם חֻקִּים,
בָּשָׂר וְדָגִים וְכָל מַטְעַמִּים.
יוֹם זֶה מְכֻבָּד מִכָּל יָמִים,
כִּי בוֹ שָׁבַת צוּר עוֹלָמִים.

לֹא תֶחְסַר כֹּל בּוֹ וְאָכַלְתָּ וְשָׂבָעְתָּ,
וּבֵרַכְתָּ אֶת יהוה אֱלֹהֶיךָ
אֲשֶׁר אָהַבְתָּ,
כִּי בֵרַכְךָ מִכָּל הָעַמִּים.
יוֹם זֶה מְכֻבָּד מִכָּל יָמִים,
כִּי בוֹ שָׁבַת צוּר עוֹלָמִים.

הַשָּׁמַיִם מְסַפְּרִים כְּבוֹדוֹ,
וְגַם הָאָרֶץ מָלְאָה חַסְדּוֹ,
רְאוּ כִּי כָל אֵלֶּה עָשְׂתָה יָדוֹ,
כִּי הוּא הַצּוּר פָּעֳלוֹ תָמִים.
יוֹם זֶה מְכֻבָּד מִכָּל יָמִים,
כִּי בוֹ שָׁבַת צוּר עוֹלָמִים.

אֵל אָדוֹן / Eil Adon

Hashem, ruler of all His creations,
  He is blessed by every person.
His greatness fills the world,
  He is surrounded by wisdom.

ה He is greater than all things that are holy,
  and is glorified above everything.
He judges with fairness and with merit,
  He is kind and He is merciful.

ט The sun, moon, stars, and planets
  that He created are good,
He formed them with His wisdom,
He gave them strength and power
  to shine over the whole world.

מ Filled with light and shining bright,
  they sparkle brightly
  throughout the world.
The sun, moon, and planets orbit around,
  they do the will of their Creator, Hashem.

פ They give His Name glory and honor,
  adding happiness and joyful song
  to His rule.
He called out to the sun and it glowed,
He created the shape of the moon.

ש Everything in the Heavens
  sings His praise,
  all His holy creations.

אֵל אָדוֹן עַל כָּל הַמַּעֲשִׂים,
בָּרוּךְ וּמְבֹרָךְ
בְּפִי כָּל נְשָׁמָה,
גָּדְלוֹ וְטוּבוֹ מָלֵא עוֹלָם,
דַּעַת וּתְבוּנָה סוֹבְבִים אוֹתוֹ.

הַמִּתְגָּאֶה עַל חַיּוֹת הַקֹּדֶשׁ,
וְנֶהְדָּר בְּכָבוֹד עַל הַמֶּרְכָּבָה,
זְכוּת וּמִישׁוֹר לִפְנֵי כִסְאוֹ,
חֶסֶד וְרַחֲמִים לִפְנֵי כְבוֹדוֹ.

טוֹבִים מְאוֹרוֹת שֶׁבָּרָא אֱלֹהֵינוּ,
יְצָרָם בְּדַעַת בְּבִינָה וּבְהַשְׂכֵּל,
כֹּחַ וּגְבוּרָה נָתַן בָּהֶם,
לִהְיוֹת מוֹשְׁלִים בְּקֶרֶב תֵּבֵל.

מְלֵאִים זִיו וּמְפִיקִים נֹגַהּ,
נָאֶה זִיוָם בְּכָל הָעוֹלָם,
שְׂמֵחִים בְּצֵאתָם וְשָׂשִׂים בְּבוֹאָם,
עוֹשִׂים בְּאֵימָה רְצוֹן קוֹנָם.

פְּאֵר וְכָבוֹד נוֹתְנִים לִשְׁמוֹ,
צָהֳלָה וְרִנָּה לְזֵכֶר מַלְכוּתוֹ,
קָרָא לַשֶּׁמֶשׁ וַיִּזְרַח אוֹר,
רָאָה וְהִתְקִין צוּרַת הַלְּבָנָה.

שֶׁבַח נוֹתְנִים לוֹ כָּל צְבָא מָרוֹם,
תִּפְאֶרֶת וּגְדֻלָּה, שְׂרָפִים וְאוֹפַנִּים
וְחַיּוֹת הַקֹּדֶשׁ —

A Closer Look
  In this prayer we say that the whole universe was created by Hashem, and everything sings His praises. This means that when we see the wisdom and perfection with which everything was made, we realize and appreciate Hashem and His wisdom and glory.
  Hashem desires to hear our prayers and the prayers of all His creations.

Did You Know??
  This prayer is written as an "acrostic." The first letter of each phrase is in alphabetical order of the *aleph-beis*.

וַיְהִי בִּנְסֹעַ / Vayehi Binso'a

Everyone stands as the *Aron Kodesh* is opened. We remain standing until the Torah is placed on the *bimah*.
It is customary to kiss the Sefer Torah as it is being carried to the *bimah*.

When the Ark would travel in the desert, Moshe would say, "Arise, Hashem, and let Your enemies be spread apart. Let those who hate You, run from You." From Zion the Torah will go forth, and the word of Hashem will go forth from Jerusalem. Blessed is He Who gave the Torah to His nation, Israel, in holiness.

וַיְהִי בִּנְסֹעַ הָאָרֹן וַיֹּאמֶר מֹשֶׁה, קוּמָה יהוה וְיָפֻצוּ אֹיְבֶיךָ וְיָנֻסוּ מְשַׂנְאֶיךָ מִפָּנֶיךָ. כִּי מִצִּיּוֹן תֵּצֵא תוֹרָה, וּדְבַר יהוה מִירוּשָׁלָיִם. בָּרוּךְ שֶׁנָּתַן תּוֹרָה לְעַמּוֹ יִשְׂרָאֵל בִּקְדֻשָּׁתוֹ.

A Closer Look
At the time of the *Beis HaMikdash*, the greatest rabbis were in Jerusalem, and Torah wisdom went from Jerusalem to the entire world.

Did You Know??
In the desert, the Mishkan would be taken apart and put back together each time the Jewish people traveled from place to place. Inside the Mishkan was the Ark and inside the Ark were the *Aseres HaDibros*. There was also a Sefer Torah at the Ark.
Zion is another name for Jerusalem.

89

אֵין כֵּאלֹהֵינוּ / *Ein Keiloheinu*

At the end of the *Mussaf* service, it is customary in many shuls for a younger child to be made the *chazzan* and lead the service.

There is nothing else like our God.
 There is nothing else like our Master.
There is nothing else like our King.
There is nothing else like our Savior.

Who can be compared to our God?
Who can be compared to our Master?
Who can be compared to our King?
Who can be compared to our Savior?

Let us thank our God.
Let us thank our Master.
Let us thank our King.
Let us thank our Savior.

אֵין כֵּאלֹהֵינוּ, אֵין כַּאדוֹנֵינוּ,
אֵין כְּמַלְכֵּנוּ, אֵין כְּמוֹשִׁיעֵנוּ.

מִי כֵאלֹהֵינוּ, מִי כַאדוֹנֵינוּ,
מִי כְמַלְכֵּנוּ, מִי כְמוֹשִׁיעֵנוּ.

נוֹדֶה לֵאלֹהֵינוּ, נוֹדֶה לַאדוֹנֵינוּ,
נוֹדֶה לְמַלְכֵּנוּ, נוֹדֶה לְמוֹשִׁיעֵנוּ.

Did You Know??
 The first letters of the first three paragraphs in Hebrew spell out the word אָמֵן.
We should make sure to say each word when we pray. Speech is what makes us different from animals who cannot speak.

90

Blessed is our God.
Blessed is our Master.
Blessed is our King.
Blessed is our Savior.

It is You Who are our God.
It is You Who are our Master.
It is You Who are our King.
It is You Who are our Savior.

It is to You that our fathers
burned incense in the *Beis HaMikdash*.

בָּרוּךְ אֱלֹהֵינוּ, בָּרוּךְ אֲדוֹנֵינוּ,
בָּרוּךְ מַלְכֵּנוּ, בָּרוּךְ מוֹשִׁיעֵנוּ.

אַתָּה הוּא אֱלֹהֵינוּ,
אַתָּה הוּא אֲדוֹנֵינוּ,
אַתָּה הוּא מַלְכֵּנוּ,
אַתָּה הוּא מוֹשִׁיעֵנוּ.

אַתָּה הוּא שֶׁהִקְטִירוּ אֲבוֹתֵינוּ לְפָנֶיךָ
אֵת קְטֹרֶת הַסַּמִּים.

אַנְעִים זְמִירוֹת / An'im Zemiros

The Ark is opened. A verse (in bold type) is said by the *chazzan*,
and the next verse (in light type) is said by the congregation.

<table>
<tr><td>

I shall write pleasant songs,
for You, Hashem,
because I want to be close to You.

My soul wants to be
protected by You,
and know all Your secrets.

Especially when I speak
about Your glory,
my heart wants to be near You.

Therefore, I sing to You
and honor Your Name.

I will talk about Your greatness,
even though I cannot see You
or understand You.

You explained a little bit
about Your glory,
through Your prophets.

They described how powerful
You are,

by telling us
what You do.

You are the only One,
and everything is part of You.

They described You
as kindly but powerful.

Kindly in judgment,
but powerful in war,

He saves us
for His sake.

He gave us the Torah
which gives us life.

Hashem loves us
and is proud of us.

Hashem is His Name,
He is King over everything.

</td><td dir="rtl">

אַנְעִים זְמִירוֹת וְשִׁירִים אֶאֱרוֹג,
כִּי אֵלֶיךָ נַפְשִׁי תַעֲרוֹג.
נַפְשִׁי חָמְדָה בְּצֵל יָדֶךָ,
לָדַעַת כָּל רָז סוֹדֶךָ.
מִדֵּי דַבְּרִי בִּכְבוֹדֶךָ,
הוֹמֶה לִבִּי אֶל דּוֹדֶיךָ.
עַל כֵּן אֲדַבֵּר בְּךָ נִכְבָּדוֹת,
וְשִׁמְךָ אֲכַבֵּד בְּשִׁירֵי יְדִידוֹת.
אֲסַפְּרָה כְבוֹדְךָ וְלֹא רְאִיתִיךָ,
אֲדַמְּךָ אֲכַנְּךָ וְלֹא יְדַעְתִּיךָ.
בְּיַד נְבִיאֶיךָ בְּסוֹד עֲבָדֶיךָ,
דִּמִּיתָ הֲדַר כְּבוֹד הוֹדֶךָ.
גְּדֻלָּתְךָ וּגְבוּרָתֶךָ, כִּנּוּ לְתֹקֶף פְּעֻלָּתֶךָ.
דִּמּוּ אוֹתְךָ וְלֹא כְּפִי יֶשְׁךָ,
וַיְשַׁוּוּךָ לְפִי מַעֲשֶׂיךָ.
הִמְשִׁילוּךָ בְּרֹב חֶזְיוֹנוֹת,
הִנְּךָ אֶחָד בְּכָל דִּמְיוֹנוֹת.
וַיֶּחֱזוּ בְךָ זִקְנָה וּבַחֲרוּת,
וּשְׂעַר רֹאשְׁךָ בְּשֵׂיבָה וְשַׁחֲרוּת.
זִקְנָה בְּיוֹם דִּין וּבַחֲרוּת בְּיוֹם קְרָב,
כְּאִישׁ מִלְחָמוֹת יָדָיו לוֹ רָב.
חָבַשׁ כּוֹבַע יְשׁוּעָה בְּרֹאשׁוֹ,
הוֹשִׁיעָה לּוֹ יְמִינוֹ וּזְרוֹעַ קָדְשׁוֹ.
טַלְלֵי אוֹרוֹת רֹאשׁוֹ נִמְלָא,
קְוֻצּוֹתָיו רְסִיסֵי לָיְלָה.
יִתְפָּאֵר בִּי כִּי חָפֵץ בִּי,
וְהוּא יִהְיֶה לִי לַעֲטֶרֶת צְבִי.
כֶּתֶם טָהוֹר פָּז דְּמוּת רֹאשׁוֹ,
וְחַק עַל מֵצַח כְּבוֹד שֵׁם קָדְשׁוֹ.

</td></tr>
</table>

Our prayers are His crown.

Hashem does not change.

He always was and always will be.

His home, the *Beis HaMikdash,*
is where His pride is greatest.
May He bring it back to the glory
it once had.

May the Jewish people be His crown,
that He is proud of.

The Jewish people are precious to Hashem,
from the very beginnings and forever.

He is near to us
when we call to Him.

He will take revenge
against the nations of the world,
who were bad to the Jewish people.

Hashem showed Moshe Rabbeinu
how dear the Jewish people
are to Him.

He desires us,
and makes humble people important.

Your word is true,
as is seen right from
the very beginning of the Torah.

Place my songs before You, Hashem.

May my praises be a crown for You,
and be accepted like the incense
in the *Beis HaMikdash.*

Let each human being's song
be dear to You,
like the prayers said over Your sacrifices
in the *Beis Hamikdash.*

Accept my prayers, Hashem,
Who gives life and is fair and powerful.

Accept my prayers
just as You would accept
sweet-smelling incense.

Let my prayers and songs
be sweet to You, Hashem,
for my soul wants to be close to You.

לְחֵן וּלְכָבוֹד צְבִי תִפְאָרָה,
אֻמָּתוֹ לוֹ עִטְּרָה עֲטָרָה.
מַחְלְפוֹת רֹאשׁוֹ כְּבִימֵי בְחֻרוֹת,
קְוֻצּוֹתָיו תַּלְתַּלִּים שְׁחוֹרוֹת.
נְוֵה הַצֶּדֶק צְבִי תִפְאַרְתּוֹ,
יַעֲלֶה נָּא עַל רֹאשׁ שִׂמְחָתוֹ.
סְגֻלָּתוֹ תְּהִי בְיָדוֹ עֲטֶרֶת,
וּצְנִיף מְלוּכָה צְבִי תִפְאֶרֶת.
עֲמוּסִים נְשָׂאָם עֲטֶרֶת עֲנָדָם,
מֵאֲשֶׁר יָקְרוּ בְעֵינָיו כִּבְּדָם.
פְּאֵרוֹ עָלַי וּפְאֵרִי עָלָיו,
וְקָרוֹב אֵלַי בְּקָרְאִי אֵלָיו.
צַח וְאָדוֹם לִלְבוּשׁוֹ אָדוֹם,
פּוּרָה בְּדָרְכוֹ בְּבוֹאוֹ מֵאֱדוֹם.
קֶשֶׁר תְּפִלִּין הֶרְאָה לֶעָנָו,
תְּמוּנַת יהוה לְנֶגֶד עֵינָיו.
רוֹצֶה בְעַמּוֹ עֲנָוִים יְפָאֵר,
יוֹשֵׁב תְּהִלּוֹת בָּם לְהִתְפָּאֵר.
רֹאשׁ דְּבָרְךָ אֱמֶת קוֹרֵא מֵרֹאשׁ,
דּוֹר וָדוֹר עַם דּוֹרֶשְׁךָ דְּרוֹשׁ.
שִׁית הֲמוֹן שִׁירַי נָא עָלֶיךָ,
וְרִנָּתִי תִקְרַב אֵלֶיךָ.
תְּהִלָּתִי תְּהִי לְרֹאשְׁךָ עֲטֶרֶת,
וּתְפִלָּתִי תִּכּוֹן קְטֹרֶת.
תִּיקַר שִׁירַת רָשׁ בְּעֵינֶיךָ,
כַּשִּׁיר יוּשַׁר עַל קָרְבָּנֶיךָ.
בִּרְכָתִי תַעֲלֶה לְרֹאשׁ מַשְׁבִּיר,
מְחוֹלֵל וּמוֹלִיד צַדִּיק כַּבִּיר.
וּבְבִרְכָתִי תְנַעֲנַע לִי רֹאשׁ,
וְאוֹתָהּ קַח לְךָ כִּבְשָׂמִים רֹאשׁ.
יֶעֱרַב נָא שִׂיחִי עָלֶיךָ,
כִּי נַפְשִׁי תַעֲרוֹג אֵלֶיךָ.

קִדּוּש / Shabbos Day Kiddush

We say the following *Kiddush* after prayers on Shabbos, before eating.

Therefore, Hashem blessed the Shabbos and made it holy.

עַל כֵּן בֵּרַךְ יהוה אֶת יוֹם הַשַּׁבָּת וַיְקַדְּשֵׁהוּ.

Please listen my masters:

סַבְרִי מָרָנָן וְרַבָּנָן וְרַבּוֹתַי:

Blessed are You, Hashem, our God, King of the universe, Who creates the fruit of the grapevine.

בָּרוּךְ אַתָּה יהוה אֱלֹהֵינוּ מֶלֶךְ הָעוֹלָם, בּוֹרֵא פְּרִי הַגָּפֶן.

Did You Know??

Two challos, called *lechem mishneh,* are placed on the table at each Shabbos meal. These two challos remind us of the two portions of the manna (מָן) that Hashem gave us every Friday when we were in the desert after leaving Egypt.

Manna was the special heavenly bread that the Jews received in the desert. No manna ever fell on Shabbos. Instead, the Jewish people received a double portion on Friday.

There are 39 basic types of work that we are not allowed to do on Shabbos.

A Closer Look
Our Sages teach us that keeping the laws of Shabbos is as important as keeping all the other laws of the Torah.

הַבְדָּלָה / *Havdalah*

When Shabbos is over, we say *Havdalah*. We use 1) a special candle which has at least two flames together, 2) a cup of wine, 3) special spices. The person reciting *Havdalah* says:

Hashem saves me from everything that is bad. I trust Him and am not afraid, because Hashem is my strength. Hashem saves me. You shall get water from the springs of salvation. Hashem can save us; may your blessings be on Your Nation. Hashem is with us, He is our strength. Praised is the person who trusts in You, Hashem. Hashem, save us. Please answer us, our King, when we call to You. There was light, happiness, joy, and honor for the Jewish people. I will raise the cup of salvation, and call out the Name of Hashem.

הִנֵּה אֵל יְשׁוּעָתִי אֶבְטַח וְלֹא אֶפְחָד, כִּי עָזִּי וְזִמְרָת יָהּ יהוה, וַיְהִי לִי לִישׁוּעָה. וּשְׁאַבְתֶּם מַיִם בְּשָׂשׂוֹן, מִמַּעַיְנֵי הַיְשׁוּעָה. לַיהוה הַיְשׁוּעָה, עַל עַמְּךָ בִרְכָתֶךָ סֶּלָה. יהוה צְבָאוֹת עִמָּנוּ, מִשְׂגָּב לָנוּ אֱלֹהֵי יַעֲקֹב סֶלָה. יהוה צְבָאוֹת, אַשְׁרֵי אָדָם בֹּטֵחַ בָּךְ. יהוה הוֹשִׁיעָה, הַמֶּלֶךְ יַעֲנֵנוּ בְיוֹם קָרְאֵנוּ. לַיְּהוּדִים הָיְתָה אוֹרָה וְשִׂמְחָה, וְשָׂשֹׂן וִיקָר, כֵּן תִּהְיֶה לָּנוּ. כּוֹס יְשׁוּעוֹת אֶשָּׂא, וּבְשֵׁם יהוה אֶקְרָא.

Please listen my masters

סַבְרִי מָרָנָן וְרַבָּנָן וְרַבּוֹתַי:

Blessed are You, Hashem, our God, King of the universe, Who creates the fruit of the grapevine.

בָּרוּךְ אַתָּה יהוה אֱלֹהֵינוּ מֶלֶךְ הָעוֹלָם, בּוֹרֵא פְּרִי הַגָּפֶן.

Everyone answers Amen.

After we say the following *berachah*, we smell the spices:

Blessed are You, Hashem, our God, King of the universe, Who creates the different kinds of spices.

בָּרוּךְ אַתָּה יהוה אֱלֹהֵינוּ מֶלֶךְ הָעוֹלָם, בּוֹרֵא מִינֵי בְשָׂמִים.

Everyone answers Amen.

After we say the following *berachah*, we hold up our fingers to the flame to see our nails by the light of the candle:

Blessed are You, Hashem, our God, King of the universe, Who creates the light of the fire.

בָּרוּךְ אַתָּה יהוה אֱלֹהֵינוּ מֶלֶךְ הָעוֹלָם, בּוֹרֵא מְאוֹרֵי הָאֵשׁ.

Everyone answers Amen.

Blessed are You, Hashem, our God, King of the universe, Who separates between the holy and the not holy, between the light and the dark, between Israel and the other nations, between the seventh day (Shabbos), and the other days of creation. Blessed are You, Hashem, Who separates between the holy and the not holy.

בָּרוּךְ אַתָּה יהוה אֱלֹהֵינוּ מֶלֶךְ הָעוֹלָם, הַמַּבְדִּיל בֵּין קֹדֶשׁ לְחוֹל, בֵּין אוֹר לְחֹשֶׁךְ, בֵּין יִשְׂרָאֵל לָעַמִּים, בֵּין יוֹם הַשְּׁבִיעִי לְשֵׁשֶׁת יְמֵי הַמַּעֲשֶׂה. בָּרוּךְ אַתָּה יהוה, הַמַּבְדִּיל בֵּין קֹדֶשׁ לְחוֹל.

Everyone answers Amen.

Whoever recited *Havdalah* should drink most of the wine, then pour some of the wine into a dish. The flame should then be put out by dipping it into the wine. It is customary to dip your fingers into the dish of wine and touch your eyelids and inner pockets with them. This reminds us that the light of this mitzvah will show us the true way of Hashem and bring us blessings the entire week.

חֲנוּכָּה / *Chanukah*

On the first night of Chanukah we say the following three *berachos*.
On each of the next nights, only the first two *berachos* are said.

Blessed are You, Hashem, our God, King of the universe, Who has made us holy with His mitzvos, and commanded us to light the Chanukah lights.

בָּרוּךְ אַתָּה יהוה אֱלֹהֵינוּ מֶלֶךְ הָעוֹלָם, אֲשֶׁר קִדְּשָׁנוּ בְּמִצְוֹתָיו, וְצִוָּנוּ לְהַדְלִיק נֵר (שֶׁל) חֲנֻכָּה.

Blessed are You, Hashem, our God, King of the universe, Who has made miracles for our fathers, in those days at this time of the year.

בָּרוּךְ אַתָּה יהוה אֱלֹהֵינוּ מֶלֶךְ הָעוֹלָם, שֶׁעָשָׂה נִסִּים לַאֲבוֹתֵינוּ, בַּיָּמִים הָהֵם בַּזְּמַן הַזֶּה.

Blessed are You, Hashem, our God, King of the universe, for keeping us alive, taking care of us, and bringing us to this time.

בָּרוּךְ אַתָּה יהוה אֱלֹהֵינוּ מֶלֶךְ הָעוֹלָם, שֶׁהֶחֱיָנוּ וְקִיְּמָנוּ וְהִגִּיעָנוּ לַזְּמַן הַזֶּה.

On the first night we light the candle on the far right. On each of the following nights, a new candle is added and lit to the left of the previous night's candle. The new candle is lit first. On the eighth night, all eight candles are lit.

Did You Know??

The candles should be lit in a place where people outside the house can also see them. This way we show the world that a great miracle occurred, and that everyone should know about it.

The Chanukah lights are holy and therefore we are not allowed to use the lights for any other purpose, such as reading.

It is customary to have an extra candle, called the *shamash*, which we use to light the other candles. The *shamash* is placed either higher or lower on the menorah than the other lights. This shows that the *shamash* is not one of the Chanukah lights. If the light of the menorah is used by mistake, then we are actually only using the *shamash*.

The Chanukah candles must stay lit for at least one half hour.

It is customary for children to play *dreidel* on Chanukah.

A Closer Look

On Chanukah we eat potato pancakes, *latkes* and fried jelly donuts. These foods are all fried in oil, and it reminds us that the miracle of Chanukah happened with oil. In the *Beis HaMikdash,* there was only enough oil for one night, but the oil burned for eight full days and nights.